PENGUIN CLASSICS

What the critics said about *Agapē Agape*

"Gaddis confronted our modern world without flinching. He mapped and delved. His reach was enormous . . . *Agapē Agape* is the deathbed summa, the parting shot—complete and fully realized . . . its every strange sentence carries full disciplined intention, hurtling towards synthesis even as it writhes and falls. . . . The book is an exalted, paranoid outcry, a last wounded proclamation of the idea of the sacred rootedness of true art . . . we bring to these pages our sense of his great authority and attainment."
            —Sven Birkerts, *The New York Times Book Review*

"An excellent prelude to the themes that so obsessed Gaddis . . . Gaddis's strengths were in creating dazzling architectures for his fictions, and in capturing the ironies and rhythms of human speech."
            —John Freeman, *The Boston Globe*

"Gaddis's final novel is perhaps his most poignant . . . the themes that obsess the novel's hero go round and round his head in a kind of discordant symphony: Plato's plot to banish poets as dangerous to the state. Freud's elevation of the pleasure principle. Bentham's utilitarian insistence on viewing pleasure as a question of quantity rather than quality."   —Merle Rubin, *Los Angeles Times*

"For Gaddis, as well as his unnamed protagonist, the player piano represents everything that has gone wrong with America. It's the perfect symbol for the mechanization of art, the death of creativity . . . it is also the novel's jumping off point, allowing the protagonist to consider everything from the history of the digital computer to Glenn Gould, to mechanical birds, to modern medicine . . . there's something on virtually every page—an idea, a turn of phrase, a bit of invective, a peculiar historical note—that stopped me for a moment. . . . In the end, the novel represents the perfect introduction to Gaddis's work and thought, having condensed a lifetime into about 100 pages (though looking at it that way, of course, would have pissed him off as well)."   —Jim Knipfel, *New York Press*

"As a glimpse into the literary impulse exercised under difficult, even mortal circumstances, *Agapē Agape* is harrowing, resolute, deeply sad, very memorable."   —Rick Moody, *Bookforum*

"A precisely cut diamond whose brilliance appears at first glance but whose myriad facets—a dance of light and shadow—multiply through reflection. . . . Gaddis rages against the world, but his novel is memorable because he channels this anger into a superb meditation on self-doubt, mortality, and the need for artists to persevere against deaf ears."   —J. Peder Zane, *The Raleigh News Observer*

"Gaddis's last blast, *Agapē Agape*, ultimately leads the reader back to *The Recognitions* itself . . . a breathless epilogue to an immense body of work, an acid tirade all too human with sentiment, *Agapē Agape* could not have cut a more affecting path back to the source, a nearly fifty-year course that affirms the ideal of the opus alchymicum, the work as self-generating recirculations. . . . It may seem to reach us *too late*, after its author's death, but it actually comes *at the proper time*: posthumously."   —Ed Park, *The Village Voice*

"A snarling jeremiad . . . the isolation of a forgotten writer, this time bedridden and moribund, preparing, Lear-like, to divide his property among his three daughters while distractedly arranging evidence of civilization's collapse garnered from various mentors and sources (among them the theoretical physicist Willard Gibbs, cultural historian Johan Huizinga, Freud, Tolstoy's bilious novella *The Kreutzer Sonata*, Svengali and Trilby, even Plato's allegory of the cave and his theory of art as the rightful possession of a cultural elite), building his argument that the player piano epitomizes the death of individuality and the triumph of meretriciousness."
          —Bruce Allen, *Kirkus Reviews*

"In his incisive, caustically elegiac final novel, Gaddis conjures up an erudite, drug-addled old gent with a terminal illness, a true monomaniac, who delivers a torrential and trenchant monologue on art versus entertainment, authenticity versus imitation, and death and the dream of art's immortality."
          —Donna Seaman, *Booklist*

"*Agapē Agape* was written by Gaddis with the understanding that it would be his last published act as an author. That crushing awareness of his own end is nearly palpable on every page. As a consequence, the writing is as deeply melancholic as it is directed. Thoughts are expressed without frills and with the utmost urgency."
          —Paul Maliszewski, *The Wilson Quarterly*

PENGUIN  CLASSICS

AGAPĒ AGAPE

WILLIAM GADDIS (1922–1998) was twice awarded the National Book Award, for his novels *J R* and *A Frolic of His Own*. His other novels were *The Recognitions* and *Carpenter's Gothic*; he was also the author of a collection of essays, *The Rush for Second Place*. He was a member of the American Academy of Arts and Letters and the recipient of a MacArthur Prize.

SVEN BIRKERTS is the author of *My Sky Blue Trades, The Gutenberg Elegies, Readings, American Energies,* and other books. He teaches at Mount Holyoke College, is a member of the core faculty of the Bennington Writing Seminars, and is the editor of the journal *Agni.* He lives in Arlington, Massachusetts.

JOSEPH TABBI is the author of *Cognitive Fictions,* a comprehensive look at the effect of new technologies on contemporary fiction, and the founding editor of *ebr,* the electronic book review. He was the first scholar to be given access to the Gaddis archives in the summer of 2001. Tabbi conducts research in American literature and new media writing at the University of Illinois at Chicago.

WILLIAM GADDIS

Agapē Agape

Introduction by SVEN BIRKERTS

Afterword by JOSEPH TABBI

PENGUIN BOOKS

PENGUIN BOOKS

Published by the Penguin Group
Penguin Group (USA) Inc., 375 Hudson Street, New York, New York 10014, U.S.A.
Penguin Books Ltd, 80 Strand, London WC2R 0RL, England
Penguin Books Australia Ltd, 250 Camberwell Road, Camberwell, Victoria 3124, Australia
Penguin Books Canada Ltd, 10 Alcorn Avenue, Toronto, Ontario, Canada M4V 3B2
Penguin Books India (P) Ltd, 11 Community Centre, Panchsheel Park,
New Delhi – 110 017, India
Penguin Books (N.Z.) Ltd, Cnr Rosedale and Airborne Roads, Albany, Auckland, New Zealand
Penguin Books (South Africa) (Pty) Ltd, 24 Sturdee Avenue,
Rosebank, Johannesburg 2196, South Africa

Penguin Books Ltd, Registered Offices:
80 Strand, London WC2R 0RL, England

First published in the United States of America by Viking Penguin,
a member of Penguin Putnam Inc., 2002
Published in Penguin Books 2003

Grateful acknowledgment is made for permission to reprint excerpts from
A Confederacy of Dunces by John Kennedy Toole. Copyright © 1980 by Thelma D. Toole.
Reprinted by permission of Louisiana State University Press.

Excerpts from *Concrete* by Thomas Bernhard, translated by David McLintock, Alfred A. Knopf,
1984, and *The Loser* by Thomas Bernhard, translated by Jack Dawson, Knopf, 1991.

PUBLISHER'S NOTE
This is a work of fiction. Names, characters, places, and incidents either are the
product of the author's imagination or are used fictitiously, and any resemblance to actual
persons, living or dead, business establishments, events, or locales is entirely coincidental.

ISBN 0-670-03131-3 (hc.)

ISBN 0 14 24.3763 8 (pbk.)
CIP data available

Set in Garamond 3 with Schneidler Initials
Designed by Carla Bolte

Contents

Introduction

Separating a writer from his work is difficult under any circumstances. With a novelist as personally reticent and artistically challenging as William Gaddis, it's almost impossible. There is no purchase. Legend and hearsay move into the crevices usually saved for biography. And how readily the man recedes into an image—a grainy mug shot, perhaps, as befits one so mysterious and threatening. After Thomas Pynchon, he is the most elusive of our masters, more a literary cipher than a known voice.

The Gaddis of my fantasies exerts a powerful and shadowy appeal: the gaunt figure with his frayed patrician-cum-Jack Palance looks; an updated Ahab in doomed assault on that most persistent of chimeras, the great American novel. Call it romantic twaddle, but these imaginings play no small part in the manufacture of reputations, and Gaddis' is all the more charged for his being so enigmatic.

I'm not sure, though, that reading the novels dispels the mystique so much as changes it, grafting upon the image of the charismatic loner that of the ambitious maker, the artist who would draw his compass line around the vast theme-a-turgy of contemporary American life. Indeed, from his first book, *The Recognitions* (1955), his monumental cosmopolitan epic of forgery and fate, to *JR* (1975), his utterly *sui generis* voice-portrait of American enterprise, to his more accessible recent novels, *Carpenter's Gothic* (1985) and *A Frolic of His Own* (1994), Gaddis declared himself unapologetically serious, a man on the way to the big synthesis.

Gaddis' enterprise was not so much a search for themes as a search for ways to weave into some strong textile all the features and elements that shape our experience—political, economic, artistic, erotic, etc. Living writers who share this aspiration—and who have certainly drawn courage from his example—include William Gass, Thomas Pynchon, Don DeLillo, Joseph McElroy, Rick Moody, Jonathan Franzen, Maureen Howard, David Foster Wallace, Richard Powers, and Cynthia Ozick. The fact that they are mostly males makes for an unfashionable list in some ways, but it also testifies to a certain machismo impetus behind the maximalist assault on the novel. I don't know how else to explain it.

There is a certain symbolic aptness in the fact that the novelist who began on such a scale—covering continents and decades with his populous plots and conspiracies—should end, as many do who live long enough, carved back to essential bone and sinew. Not "sans teeth," and not "sans everything," but very much sans elaboration. *Agapē Agape,* the unstructured monologue of a man living through his last days, would seem to be the antipodean Gaddis, his minimalist rejoinder to the vast accumulations that preceded it. But as we will see, it is also a continuation of the arc of the work and its fitting terminus.

To get the first orienting exposure to Gaddis' method, his literary aesthetic, the reader needs only a strong thumb. Fanning through the first four novels, the manual exertion easing somewhat as the bulk thins from the thousand-plus pages of *The Recognitions* to the merely gargantuan *JR,* to the more conventionally graspable two works that followed, we are struck by the relentless visual punctuation of the dash, the author's Joyce-derived way of indicating dialogue, as in this random example from *JR*:

—What? Oh I . . .

—Well what are you doing hiding in the closet

—No I'm looking for some clothes, I just . . .

—Why don't you put the closet light on then. (316)

And it goes on this way for pages at a stretch.

If nothing else, this riffling of pages vividly discloses the extent to which Gaddis centered his narratives around transcriptions of the spoken voice—voices in combat and accord; voices vigorously staking out airspace, parrying, muscling for attention and advantage. The classic instance of this is *JR,* quite possibly the most spoken book in our literature, where the characters offer their lines with what can be a frustrating lack of identifying cues, often with nothing more than syncopation and subtle telltale recurrences to help the reader to differentiate between them. I was told by one Gaddis-adept that reading that novel was a swim-or-drown proposition, that to strive for exact coordinates was to court madness; that the only way to hold the sense was by moving forward in great gulps, and trusting the plot to come clear by degrees.

But *JR* is just the extreme instance. The other three novels each in their way ask that we convert the eye-beam exertion of reading into a highly tuned-up form of listening. And when we do, we can, to crib from our founding bard, "hear America singing." Except that this singing is really anything but. What we really hear is America cajoling, scheming, grieving, complaining, disputing, lying, seducing, explaining, litigating . . . It makes perfect sense that Gaddis was a great admirer of the work of Saul Bellow, in whose pages we likewise quicken to the many strains of the endless and ongoing daily American conversation.

Which brings us, interestingly enough, to *Agapē Agape,* Gaddis' thin-yet-crowded, posthumous-yet-intended last novel. Fanning through—the process takes less than six seconds, I timed it—we discover not a single dash in the margins. Fanning again—and one more time for confirmation—we note that there is also not a single paragraph indentation, not even at the very beginning. Doubtless there are other works in the modern canon that proceed thus, but I thought right away of Thomas Bernhard's *Concrete,* and the association proved to be the right one—Gaddis in fact meant *Agapē Agape* to be an homage to Bernhard and, particularly, to that work.

Before turning to Gaddis' novel, though, I would linger

for a moment on this one peculiarity of presentation, the fact that with this unfenestrated brickwork of prose—his last work—the author effects a complete reversal of the narrative ambition of *The Recognitions,* his first. Where those pages assembled a cast, a mob, of characters, moving them around in space and in time, this pared-down monologue cuts the anchoring line to the world at large and steps entirely into the vocalized thoughts of a dying man. It tells no story, orchestrates no conflicts except those that the narrator wages in his own embattled psyche—mainly between the given and the desired, the harsh grain of things and the vision of art that might redeem it. Yet paradoxically, where the big novels always seem to telegraph the unstated promise of the world they are rooted in—thus carrying a sense of yet unfilled spaces—*Agapē Agape* feels full to the brim with the pulsations of its inner life.

It will not do, I think, to consider *Agapē Agape* as simply the fifth and last of Gaddis' novels. There is an enormous subjective—psychological and metaphysical—difference between a book written as a book, for itself, as it were, and one written with the author's apprehension of his own death. The pressure to make it a summa of some kind, a last word, has to be enormous. In Gaddis' case that pressure dictated both the narrative conception—that these are the thoughts of a dying man—and the style, which is not only swift with the urgency of "last days," but which palpably maps the jittery shifts of consciousness caused by the prednisone he takes for his cancer. How fitting that Gaddis should have claimed and incorporated Bernhard's short novel as his shadow text; *Concrete,* too, surges with a literally mortal velocity, and also rides the prednisone-agitated states of its first-person narrator, Rudolph. But with this one all-important difference: Bernhard's Rudolph is a device, the stand-in voice of a writer still some years from his own untimely death. Gaddis' voice, if not point-for-point his own, is yet calculated to be close enough to generate the core tension of the work.

The near superimposition of fictional identity upon the real intensifies the immediacy of the voice—its hold-you-fast-by-the-shirtfront quality—even as it has us hunting for correlations with what we know, or can easily find out, about the author. Primarily, of course, there is the fact that he was himself dying of cancer as he wrote his dying narrator. (Gaddis died in 1998, soon after finishing *Agapē Agape.*) But the few autobiographical references we get further confirm a near-identification of author and narrator. Among these, the most salient is the narrator's long-standing obsession with the history of the player piano that he has been writing. Gaddis himself had just such a project underway for many years, as the excerpts gathered in his posthumous collection of pieces, *The Rush for Second Place,* attest. What's more, the writing of just such a history occupies his character Jack Gibbs in *JR,* which should alert us to the fact that the author long made free with the materials of his own experience in his fiction.

Gaddis all along had more in mind, however, than just documenting a particular interlude in the history of applied mechanization. The player piano was for him a significantly symbolic development and its history illuminated a great deal about the growth of binary thinking and what he saw as the epochal shift from artistic to entertainment values. In this way it lends itself perfectly to his several linked larger investigations, including the questioning of the authenticity and authority of artistic work (*The Recognitions*) and the warping force of capitalism (*JR*), especially in the cultural arena. His views often recall those expressed by Walter Benjamin in his great essay, "The Work of Art in the Age of Mechanical Reproduction," which weighed the loss of "aura"—the immediacy of the unique work of art—against the proclaimed gains of a democratic dissemination of reproductions.

But of course Walter Benjamin got there first. Moreover, Benjamin mounted a sustained argument, whereas Gaddis' treatment, either via Jack Gibbs, in his voluminous notes, or in his protagonist's drug-inflected musings in *Agapē Agape,* was impressionistic at best. He used his research to make what is finally an emotional argument about the decline of culture, the compromise of quality and uniqueness by lock-step standardization and the popular ethos of relativism. Still, the serious intellectual grounding is there and his critique lends considerable power to this transcription of a dying man's outcry.

Gaddis begins: "No but you see I've got to explain all this because I don't, we don't know how much time there is left and I have to work on the, to finish this work of mine while I, why I've brought in this whole pile of books notes pages

clippings and God knows what, get it all sorted and organized when I get this property divided up and the business
and worries that go with it while they keep me here to be cut
up and scraped." And from here the prose pushes on, without
pauses or rests, gathering and losing momentum as the narrator's thought-fugue plays itself out.

The writing plunges us straightaway into the distressed
mind-state of a dying man. It is, on that level, mimetic. It is
also complexly calculated. Aside from the obvious debt to the
stream-of-consciousness strains of modernism (James Joyce
and Virginia Woolf), we can point to the click-and-rewind
line disruptions of Samuel Beckett, most obviously in *Krapp's
Last Tape,* and the staggered syncopations of the player piano
itself, or of Glenn Gould (invoked admiringly in these pages)
imposing his peculiar discipline on the idea of the melodic.
But the true root influence remains Bernhard's disturbing
novel *Concrete,* and Gaddis' incorporation of the Austrian
master deserves our attention, not least because in the process
of invoking him he more or less offers us a cross section view
of both his procedure and his themes.

The key passage comes early in the book. The narrator—
he is in the hospital—has already begun to inveigh against
the proliferation of the player piano: ". . . it was the plague,"
he states, "spreading across America a hundred years ago with
its punched paper roll at the heart of the whole thing, of the
frenzy of invention and mechanization and democracy and
how to have art without the artist and automation, cybernetics, you can see where the damn!" The exclamation does not

signal the end of the thought by any means. It merely marks a shift of focus—the narrator has suddenly discovered that he is bleeding. By this point we are already schooled in the jerky disruptions of the style, how they signal abrupt swerves of consciousness. We tune in as he resumes, almost detached: ". . . blood all over the place it doesn't hurt no, skin's like parchment that's the prednisone, turns the skin into dry old parchment tear it open with a feather that's the prednisone, reach for a book reach for anything tear myself to pieces reaching for this book listen, you'll see what I mean, opening page you'll see what I mean," whereupon—and now we must pay very close attention—he shifts again, this time moving directly into the translated prose of Bernhard. The narrator now enfolds the opening sentence of *Concrete*—never directly identified as such—into his own thought, connecting Bernhard's words directly to the preceding, as follows: "'From March to December,' he says, 'while I was having to take large quantities of prednisolone,' same thing as prednisone, 'I assembled every possible book and article written by' you see what I mean? 'and visited every possible and impossible and impossible library' this whole pile of books and papers here? 'preparing myself with the most passionate seriousness for the task, which I had been dreading throughout the preceding winter, of writing' . . ."

Gaddis has never been what we could call "reader-friendly." Indeed, if his own staggering, impacted style were not enough, he must tax us further with the stitched in phrases of another equally disjunctive, headlong stylist. His homage. But then, a few sentences farther on, he exclaims: "It's my opening page, he's plagiarized my work right here in front of me before I've even written it!" (p. 12). What a wonderful, addled, utterly appropriate move, to fuse paranoia and idolatry into a preemptive reversal, the borrower accusing the originator of taking his words before he's written them. It wouldn't stand up in a court of law, but damn the logic—it's the fondest soldering of sensibilities that happens here, or, to vary the metaphor, a kind of literary author-pophagy. And the point of the alliance? To me it betokens a strategy of acceleration and intensification. If a poet wants to offer a lyric memorial, she reaches for the elegy form. Just so, when Gaddis, a novelist, would speak from the edge of extinction, he seizes on a precedent. And not just any precedent—after all, he could have used Hermann Broch's *The Death of Virgil,* Marguerite Yourcenar's *Hadrian's Memoirs,* Carlos Fuentes' *The Death of Artemio Cruz,* and doubtless many others—but that of Bernhard, the fierce, enraged, principled, scornful, headlong denouncer of Western decline, the author who can scarcely speak for the contending pressure of his many vituperations.

Yes, Gaddis' dying protagonist is enraged, and as he says himself: "all writing worth reading comes, like suicide, from outrage or revenge" (p. 63). It is a pronouncement we may not entirely endorse, but in this context we do paid heed, for Gaddis' novel is fueled on many levels by the darker emotions. Primarily, of course, *Agapē Agape* is a lacerating cry against bodily pain and death—the man is actively suffering.

And his suffering puts the edge on the big questions, the old questions. In the absence of plot, they are what survives. What has my life been? What is in store? What is the point of our strife and toiling—the very questions raised by Tolstoy (who is invoked often in these pages) in *The Death of Ivan Ilych* and elsewhere. And so we find the author interrogating everything, blasting corruption and cowardice, inveighing against bodily dissolution with one breath and the timorousness of literary prize committees with the next.

But a novel, even a novel that is basically a deathbed screed, cannot just rail indiscriminately at one thing and another. It needs a center, a more directed thrust. This is where the player piano comes in, supplying the framework for the larger, more abstract obsessions. We are alerted to these right away as Gaddis declares his preoccupation and his stance: ". . . that's what my work is about, the collapse of everything, of meaning, of language, of values, of art, disorder and dislocation wherever you look, entropy drowning everything in sight, entertainment and technology and every four year old with a computer, everybody his own artist where the whole thing came from, the binary system and the computer where technology came from in the first place, you see?" If we don't at first, we do by the time he has concluded his rant.

To begin to approach what Gaddis intended, we might take a moment to parse the novel's most peculiar title A-GAH-PE A-GAPE. Five syllables, two languages and an oxymoronic opposition of meanings. The first word—from the Greek—has religious meaning, as Gaddis reminds us; it refers to "that natural merging of created life in this creation in love that transcends it, a celebration of the love that created it." "Agape," meanwhile, which has embedded in it the word "gap," carries the customary meaning of something cleft or opened. A wholeness torn asunder, then, a fall away from origins.

The idea of the gap is relevant here, for Gaddis' great interest in the player piano—which clearly has literal as well as emblematic application—is focused on the gap-filled piano roll, which, along with Joseph Marie Jacquard's early nineteenth-century punch-card loom, is seen as a forerunner of the on-off switch simplifications of binary-based systems, and therefore closely linked, at least theoretically, to the eventual emergence of cyberculture.

This is, yes, a great deal to push together, certainly a great deal to lay at the feet—or pedals—of the piano player. But this is how an intelligence like Gaddis' works—finding examples, interrogating premises, and extrapolating outward until a whole world picture starts to come into focus.

Or attempted focus, in this case, for Gaddis' narrator is so enraged, so pill distracted (remember the tone of that opening sentence), so chaotically submerged in his notes and papers that we never get a sustained or lucid argument. We grasp that the player piano appeared in the late nineteenth century, putting applied mechanization in the service of popular entertainment; that it brought the finest fruits of popular culture to the paying masses; that it was a way of "having art without the artist because he's a threat, because the creative artist has to be a threat so he's swamped by the performer." The sentences here propagate feverishly, treating the instrument not as a tool so much as a symbolic expression of deeply-rooted cultural tendencies, examining it in the light of ultimates, *sub specie aeternitatis,* as it were, building assertions and implications until we finally get to a citation from the philosopher Democritus about how "the finest poems were composed with 'inspiration and a holy breath' . . . the holy breath that sets us apart from reason and above reason, some inner revelation, some inner ecstasy even some abnormal mental state why they're out to eliminate us."

The declaration brings relief and clarification. Here, at last, Gaddis sets out the terms of the opposition and links art, at least at its foundations, to the almost hermetic traditions of spirit. The passage—and indeed the book—is now revealed to be an exalted, paranoid outcry, a last proclamation of the idea of the sacred rootedness of true art. In this way, *Agapē Agape* looks back to *The Recognitions,* to Gaddis' fascination with authenticity and the originating impulse of creativity.

As must be evident by now, Gaddis is no aesthetic democrat. He is an unapologetic elitist, very likely a subscriber to the long-banished—but in certain quarters (most recently in the work of Harold Bloom) recrudescent—idea of artist as genius innovator. From Democritus and the "holy breath" he bends his thought back to his own situation, reconnecting with his animus: ". . . why they'd say I'm afraid of the death of the elite because it means the death of me of course I can't really blame them, I've been wrong about everything in my life it's all been fraud and fiction . . ."

His is a dark brooding, and more than a little wounded:

"Fact that I'm forgotten that I'm left on the shelf with the dead white guys in the academic curriculum that my prizes are forgotten because today everybody's giving prizes for that supine herd out there waiting to be entertained, try to educate them did they buy those 'Educator' piano rolls teach them to play with their hands no, went right on discovering their unsuspected talent playing with their feet here's Flaubert's yes, 'The entire dream of democracy' he says, 'is to raise the proletariat to the level of bourgeois stupidity.'"

Agapē Agape is not in any sense of the word a happy book. Nor, indeed, is it in any strict sense a novel. A thinly veiled autobiographical rant does not a fiction make. But—and the conjunction here is critical—the book is something more than the sum of its execrations. It is a brimstone tract, but it is also art. The voice holds fast, draws us back and forth over the art/life boundary with relentless insistence, while Gaddis' artifice of giving his thoughts and howls of outrage to a dying writer imparts the eerie feeling that these are really the author's own deathbed apprehensions of the darker truths of life. Whether we have read Gaddis' oeuvre or not, we bring to these pages our sense of his great authority and attainment. These are not just any lamentations. They are Gaddis' "mene, mene, tekel, upharsin"—we have been weighed in the balance and we have been found wanting—inscribed under obvious duress. The artist's hard-won insights are driven home with a shudder.

Agapē Agape

No but you see I've got to explain all this because I don't, we don't know how much time there is left and I have to work on the, to finish this work of mine while I, why I've brought in this whole pile of books notes pages clippings and God knows what, get it all sorted and organized when I get this property divided up and the business and worries that go with it while they keep me here to be cut up and scraped and stapled and cut up again my damn leg look at it, layered with staples like that old suit of Japanese armour in the dining hall feel like I'm being dismantled piece by piece, houses, cottages, stables orchards and all the damn decisions and distractions I've got the papers land surveys deeds and all of it right in this heap somewhere, get it cleared up and settled before everything collapses and it's all swallowed up by lawyers and taxes like everything else because that's what it's about, that's what my work is about, the collapse of everything, of meaning, of language, of values, of art, disorder and dislocation wherever you look, entropy drowning everything in sight, entertainment and technology and every four year old with a computer, everybody his own artist where the whole thing came from, the binary system and the computer where technology came from in the first place, you see? I can't even go into it, you see that's what I have to go into before all my work is misunderstood and distorted and, and turned into a cartoon because it is a cartoon, whole stupefied mob out there waiting to be entertained, turning the creative artist into a performer, into a celebrity like Byron, the man in the place of his work when probability came in and threw that whole safe predictable Newtonian world into chaos, into disorder wherever you turn, discontinuity, disparity, difference, discord, contradiction, what they're calling aporia they took from the Greeks, the academics took the word from the Greeks for this swamp of ambiguity, paradox, perversity, opacity, obscurity, anarchy the clock without the clockmaker and the desperate comedy of Kierkegaard's insane Knight of Belief and even Pascal's famous wager in a world where everyone is "so necessarily mad that not to be mad would amount to another form of madness" where the artist is today, the artist the real artist Plato warned us about, the threat to society and the, read Huizinga on Plato and music and the artist as dangerous and art as dangerous and music in this mode and that mode, the Phrygian mode to quiet you down and the tenor and bass Lydian to make you sad and the soft and drinking harmonies, the Lydian and the Ionian where the art the, the artist having trouble breathing here I, coming out of the anaesthesia down in the recovery room tried to raise my leg and it suddenly jumped up by itself like a, like the pain avoiding pain that's what all this is about isn't it? Seeking pleasure and avoiding pain, beyond the pleasure principle? My golden Sigi his mother always called him, if Emerson was right and we are what our mothers made us? "Pleasure and pain I maintain to be the first perceptions of children," the first forms virtue and vice take for them, not my golden Sigi no, he lifted it from Plato's Laws Book II, talking about his own high ethical standards. "I subscribe to a high ideal," he tells Reverend Oskar Pfister "from which most of the human beings I have come across depart most lamentably." And then just to make clear what

little he's found that's good about these human beings, he tells Reverend Oskar Pfister "In my experience most of them are trash," probably lost sight of
their purposes never had any in the first place but
pleasure and along comes Bentham with "Pushpin is
as good as poetry if the quantity of pleasure given is
the same" see that word quantity? The quantity of
pleasure not the quality the whole point of it and
these digital machines come in, the all-or-none machine Norbert Wiener called it, machine that counts
brings in the binary system and the computer with
it, so Wiener tells us about a brilliant American engineer who's gone out and bought an expensive
player piano. Pushpin or Pushkin, doesn't care a damn
for the music but he's fascinated by the complicated
mechanism that produces it that's what America was
all about, what mechanization was all about, what
democracy was all about and the deification of
democracy a hundred years ago all this technology at
the service of entertaining Sigi's stupefied pleasure
seeking trash out there playing the piano with its
feet where it all came from isn't it? That all-or-none
paper roll with holes in it, 40,000 player pianos built
in 1909, almost 200,000 ten years later if ever the
daughters of music were brought low I mean that's

4

what I'm trying to explain, dividing the properties three ways one for each daughter all settled ahead of time before the lawyers and taxes swallow it up in dislocation and disorder getting it organized the only way to defend it against this tide of entropy that's spread everywhere since the year the player piano came into being from some Civil War battlefield like Christ, its American inventor said, and its own received it not since Willard Gibbs showed us the tendency for entropy to increase, nature's tendency to degrade the organized and destroy the meaningful when he pulled the rug out from under Newton's compact tightly organized universe with his papers on statistical physics in 1876, laid the way for this contingent universe where order is the least probable and chaos the most introducing probability and chance convinced Wiener it was not Einstein or Planck or Heisenberg but Willard Gibbs who brought on the first great revolution in twentieth century physics but that's not what I'm talking about is it, that's not what I'm trying to explain, no. No where did the, in a folder in this heap somewhere on the theory of wait wait wait, good God the whole pile spilling never get it together again I'd be, I'd be finished, lungs are gone and what's happening down below is nobody's business, metastasized into the bone why I haven't a day to waste, get the properties settled on all three of them with all the headaches that go with it and I'll stay with them by turns, four months with each daughter working on this project because I've got to get a contract and some advance money so I can finish it before I, before the, you see what I mean, before what it's about, before it all turns into what it's about. Where is it, this swamp of ambiguity, paradox, anarchy they're calling aporia his book right here somewhere probably at the bottom of the pile it was a game they played, the Greeks, a game you couldn't win, nobody could win, a parlour game proposing questions there was no clear answer to so winning wasn't the point of it no, no that's ours isn't it, right on the money because that's what the game is, the only game in town because that's what America's wait, little card there falling on the, there! You see? Whole stack of papers here organizing my research here it is, what I was looking for exactly what I'm talking about, 1927, getting the whole chronology in order 1876 to 1929 when the player piano world and everything else collapsed, the first public demonstration of television the image of the dollar sign was projected for sixty seconds by Philo T Farnsworth in 1927, see how I've got everything organized here put my finger right on it? Coming events cast their shadows and all the rest of it for Sigi's stupefied trash out there gaping at television dollar sign's all they see where we are today aren't we? Waiting to be entertained because that's where it started and that's where it ends up, avoiding pain and seeking pleasure play the piano with your feet, play cards, play pool play pushpin here it is, here's Huizinga talking about music and play he quotes Plato yes, here. "That which has neither utility nor truth nor likeness nor yet, in its effects, is harmful, can best be judged by the criterion of the charm that is in it, and by the pleasure it affords. Such pleasure, entailing as it does no appreciable good or ill, is play," goes on about little children and animals can't keep still, always moving making noise playing skipping leaping making a racket ends up where it started with toys, toys, toys, every four year old with a computer. Press buttons it lights up different colours he's supposed to be learning what, how to spell? No, it corrects his spelling doesn't need to know how to spell, how to multiply divide get the square root of God knows what don't have to read music know a cleft from a G string just keep pumping because that's where it came from like Wiener's engineer, not the music but how it's made, tubes bellows hammers the whole digital machine, whole binary system that all-or-none paper roll with the holes in it running over the tracker bar that's where all of it came from, toys and entertainment where technology comes from going back, back, back to Vaucanson's duck that ruffled its feathers and quacked waddled and shat, back a thousand, two thousand years with the penny-in-the-slot machines and water organs Hero of Alexandria made to entertain the locals and the living statues on the island of Rhodes Pindar talks about, the artificial trees and singing birds made for the Emperor of Byzantium a thousand years ago nothing but toys and games wherever you went, Charles V's armed puppets playing trumpets and drums and a lifesize singing canary made for Marie Antoinette made it pretty clear who this frivolous entertainment was for, artificial birds singing real birdsongs to teach birds how to sing? Mozart writing music for fluteplaying clocks and Beethoven's Wellington's Victory written for Maelzel's panharmonicon while those rococo Swiss watchmakers were still busy making princely gifts of musical snuff boxes and pastorals featuring tiny figures doing farm chores and the French libeled as usual for smutty versions available across the way where Vaucanson's foul duck and his shepherd boy played twenty songs on a pipe with one hand and beat a drum with the other and his flutist, good God Vaucanson's flutist! actually played the flute? Because that's where it came from, where the technology came from right down to that paper roll with the holes in it where the computer came from, you see? Just take a minute to explain all this computer madness besotted by science besotted by technology by this explosion of progress and the information revolution what we're really besotted by is people making millions, making billions from computer chips computer circuitry computer programs one man making thirty billion dollars in a year because that's what we've always been besotted by, Philo T Farnsworth had it right seventy years ago didn't he? What America's all about, what it's always been about that thirty billion dollars? What the computer's all about what all of it's all about, movie stars, ball players, what science is all about, try to pin it on some humble genius so Pascal shows up age nineteen with his digital adding machine, Leibniz with one that multiplies and divides and finally Babbage and his Difference Engine,

Babbage and his Analytical Engine with its punched cards Babbage the grandfather of the modern computer so it's Babbage Babbage Babbage but he got his idea from Jacquard's loom so that's all you ever hear, Jacquard's loom Jacquard's loom Jacquard's loom hits you square in the belly no where did I, can't believe it I just saw it here Flaubert, Flaubert must have been alphabetic with Farnsworth everything organized here it is yes here it is, letter from Flaubert 1868 asks about the silk weavers in Lyons, work in low-ceilinged rooms? in their homes? children work too? "The weaver working at a Jacquard loom" he says he's heard "is continually struck in the stomach by the shaft of the roller on which the cloth is being wound, it is the roller itself that strikes him?" There, you see? That was the factory Vaucanson had set up near Lyons that fell into disrepair and Jacquard shows up later, picks up the pieces of Vaucanson's mechanical loom for figured silks, glues the pieces together and we've got Jacquard's loom but that's not what I'm talking about, no, no it's the principle of the thing, eighty years before Babbage, it's the same principle Vaucanson used for his flutist, this drum pierced with holes and levers controlling its fingers and lip and tongue movements the air supply driven through the lips against the edge of the holes in the flute it was actually playing the notes selected by the holes in the drum, the notes selected by the holes in that roll of paper because the piano was the epidemic, it was the plague spreading across America a hundred years ago with its punched paper roll at the heart of the whole thing, of the frenzy of invention and mechanization and democracy and how to have art without the artist and automation, cybernetics you can see where the, damn! Where the tissues, just get cold water on it stop the bleeding, you see? Scrape my wrist against this drawer corner tears the skin open blood all over the place it doesn't hurt no, skin's like parchment that's the prednisone, turns the skin into dry old parchment tear it open with a feather that's the prednisone, reach for a book reach for anything tear myself to pieces reaching for this book listen, you'll see what I mean, opening page you'll see what I mean, "From March to December" he says, "while I was having to take large quantities of prednisolone," same thing as prednisone, "I assembled every possible book and article written by" you see what I mean? "and visited every possible and impossible library" this whole pile of books and papers here? "preparing myself with the most passionate seriousness for the task, which I had been dreading throughout the preceding winter, of writing" where am I here, yes, "a major work of impeccable scholarship. It had been my intention to devote the most careful study to all these books and articles and only then, having studied them with all the thoroughness the subject deserved, to begin writing my work, which I believed would leave far behind it and far beneath it everything else, both published and unpublished" you see what this is all about? "I had been planning it for ten years and had repeatedly failed to bring it to fruition," but of course you don't no, no that's the whole point of it! It's my opening page, he's plagiarized my work right here in front of me before I've even written it! That's not the only one. That's not the only one either, he's done it before, or after, word for word right in this heap somewhere you could call plagiary a kind of entropy in there corrupting the creation it's right in here somewhere I can never find anything in this mess never get it sorted out, never get it in any kind of order but that's what it's all about in the first place isn't it? Get things in order that's half the battle in fact it is the battle, organize what's essential and throw out the rest of it that's the, Phidias? For me an image slumbers in the stone who's that, Nietzsche? Probability, chance, disorder and breakdown here's that punched paper roll holding the the, damn! Getting blood all over these pages of ads for what I just said didn't I? Whole thing turns into a cartoon? an animated cartoon? Chance and disorder sweeping in and this binary system digital machine with its all-or-none paper roll holding the fort yes it was the fort, whole point of it to order and organize to eliminate chance, to eliminate failure because we've always hated failure in America like some great character flaw what technology's all about, music entertainment counting, counting, seventy years ago one great pianist cutting a roll coordinating his hands and pedaling within a fiftieth of a second 1926 one company cut and sold ten million rolls whole thing turns into a cartoon, mob out there crash bang storming the gates seeking pleasure democracy scaling the walls terrifying the elite who've had a corner on high class entertainment back to Marie Antoinette storming the Bastille with here yes, here's one yes, here's a German ad 1926 holding the line for the class act against here they come, here they come, "a still larger class of people who cannot successfully operate the usual type of player, because they lack a true sense of musical values. They have no 'ear for music,' and for that reason they play atrociously upon pianos equipped even with high grade player actions" talking about the class act? about defending these elitist music lovers? Not here no, talking about what we're always talking about. Sales! "Hence, too often, potential sales in a neighborhood are killed by someone unable to do justice to the possibilities of the player-piano he has purchased. To reach the enormous markets of the non-musical and half-musical and to conquer the growing prejudice of the truly musical" what are we going to do, educate this pleasure seeking rabble? There's Plato again agreeing that the excellence of music is measured by pleasure, but for this gang out there playing You're a Dog-gone Daisy Girl with its feet? Good God no, for them Plato rhymes with tomato, it can't be the pleasure of chance persons, he says, it's got to be music that delights the best educated or you get your poets composing to please the bad taste of their judges and finally the audience instructing each other and that's what this glorious democracy's all about isn't it? Tried to sell sets of "Educator" piano rolls eleven-fifty for a hundred thirty two lessons to teach them how to play the piano with their hands nothing doing no, no, here's one, here's what they wanted. "You can play better by roll than many who play by hand" you see? "And you can play all pieces while they can play but a few. And now even untrained persons can do it," breaks your heart. "The biggest thrill in music is playing it yourself. It's your own participation that rouses your emotions most," whole thing breaks your heart, here's another. "Retains its artistic 'feel' indefinitely," goes back to the turn of the century before the player piano, when it was still the piano player, big thing you wheeled up to the piano same punched roll it played on the keys with wooden fingers, tiny felt-tipped wooden fingers playing Scarlatti, Bach, Haydn "and old Handel. Unhappy Schubert speaks to them in the sweet tones of Rosamunde. Beethoven, master of masters, thrills alike" right on to Chopin bemoaning the fate of Poland and breathing "the fiery valor of his countrymen in Polonaise" and here's Debussy and Grieg giving testimonials. "Many of the artists will never play again, but their phantom hands will live forever" there that's what it's about, no more wooden fingers but phantom hands. "What stands between you and the music of the masters?" and then "If you were playing the 'Pilgrims' Chorus,' how much would it mean to you to have the composer, Wagner himself, by your side?" Good God! "great Wagner comes and, lifting them aloft above the clouds, transports them to the mighty Halls of old Walhalla, in Ride of Walkyries, or takes them to the cool, green depths of classic Rhine in Nibelungen Ring" standing beside you? Be terrified, if you had any sense you'd be terrified, no more wooden fingers here's the phantom hands at the keyboard, here. "If Beethoven could be heard by us today playing his sonatas" lucky he was deaf he'd, blood on the, look at that, arm right down to my hand veins look ready to burst no more tiny felt-tipped wooden fingers no, see what breaks your heart? "Science has perfected absolute pianistic reproduction" read Trilby, end up with a physiologist named Johannes Müller tried for a melody by blowing air through a real human larynx prepared with strings and weights for the muscle action thought opera companies would buy them because opera stars' fees were getting so high like they are now, like all of it is now, what happened? What happened! Go back to that biggest thrill in music is your own participation where did it tip, where did it go from participating even in these cockeyed embraces with Beethoven and Wagner and, and Hofmann and Grieg and these ghostly hands on the, what took it from entertaining to being entertained? From this phantom entertainer to this bleary stupefied pleasure seeking, what breaks your heart. "Discover your unsuspected talent" that's what breaks your heart, losing that whole, the loss of a kind of innocence that crept in, drifting away of that romantic intoxication that was really quite ridiculous but it was, no it was really quite wonderful, for the first time music in homes anyone's home "every member of the household may be a performer" this ad says, discovering his unsuspected talent with his feet, this romantic illusion of participating, playing Beethoven yourself that was being destroyed by the technology that had made it possible in the first place, the mechanization exploding everywhere and the phantom hands the, Kannst du mich mit Genuss betrügen yes that, If I ever say to the moment don't go! Verweile doch! du bist so schön! no match for the march of science that made it possible, marches right on and leaves it in the dust, pianos nobody can play and millions of piano rolls left in the dust while their splendid phantom hands are pushed further from reach by the gramophone and finally paralyzed by the radio teaching birds to sing birdsongs O God, O God, O God, Chi m'a tolto a me stesso that's

Michelangelo, that's from my book, Ch'a me fusse più presso O più di me potessi that's in my book, who has taken from me that self who could do more, and what is your book about Mister Joyce? It's not about something Madam, it is something and goodbye to that hidden talent, those ghostly fingers hard as petrified wood look at mine, the all-or-none ranks of order in those dusty piano rolls become chips in gigantic computer systems whose operators are at the mercy of the systems they've designed, programmed stock trading and the market crashes, shoot down a dot on the wrong part of the screen that was an airliner full of pleasure seekers fleeing pain and this grand billion byte technology solving every conceivable problem becomes the heart of the problem itself good God it's all, all, nuclear power going to change the world now what do we do with the nuclear waste, the waste, tiny felt-tipped wooden fingers turned to stone look at mine, keep my hands still here a few spots veins like Caesar crossing the Apennines didn't he? Blood splashed here and there you'd never know, all look perfectly normal don't I? sound perfectly normal don't I? Talking about the, about what I was talking about little hole in the memory sometimes cross out this hospital bed see me sitting here on a white sofa, white armchair books and papers in front of me? Getting old your only refuge is your work, can't see the bone scan can't see the needle in the vein drip drip God knows what hour after hour new treatment down below to strip the romantic veil off the naked animal's only function to perpetuate the species the race the tribe the, down in the recovery room leg jumps up by itself not mine no, don't dare stand up like horses the legs go first and darlin yer dancin days are done like the, book right here a minute ago like Huizinga's kangaroo just reading it wasn't I? Can't see across the room everything's a blur that's the prednisone so they're testing the eyes but I can read can't I, up close read ten point eight point but the, the, standing up just standing up take two steps I can't I can't I, I can't it's the, not my leg jumping up it's the kangaroo, it's the savage doing the magic ritual kangaroo dance he is the kangaroo, one of them has become the other, he doesn't know words, doesn't know image and symbol, doesn't know belief from make-believe Huizinga says, he has become the other and the other is the, the other has taken him over when I stand up and I I, I am the other, take two steps I can't breathe can't stand can't sp, speak can't walk across the the, I can't I can't I can't! Got to stop it's got to end right here can't breathe the other can't speak can't cross the room can't breathe can't, can't go on and I'm, I am the other. I am the other. Not the two of us living side by side like the, like some Golyadkin he invented in a bad moment no, no not those Zwei Seelen wohnen, ach! in meiner Brust one wants to leave its brother, one clings to the earth the other in derber Liebeslust no, no no no, can't breathe can't walk can't stand I am the other. Flight of stairs hold on terrified, into the bathroom the tub the toilet terrified, open the refrigerator bend down and look inside terror just, just terror where's Dodds, should have made two piles here to begin with, one books and articles and papers and clippings that are absolutely necessary the other those that aren't absolutely necessary, thought I knew which books and articles and notes were more necessary for my work than Dodds, that's the pile Dodds would be in but not damn! No, no here he is again! Right there my words right there my idea he's there ahead of me before I've even got it written down. He even writes about it this thinking another man's thoughts, put me in danger of deadening myself out of existence that's his phrase I simply haven't existed since I couldn't manage to think my own thoughts because my thinking had actually been his thinking you see? Following his thinking wherever it went so my thinking was always wherever his thinking had taken him those are my, those are his own words so I was in no condition to do anything not that I'd ever really done anything with this respiratory condition I'd had for so long even that wasn't mine treating it with prednisone while the side effects being bloated by too much prednisone while he'd cut it down or stopped it losing weight and gone back to large doses when I'd cut it down till I'd lost half my weight and he was getting bloated again the day I came I thought this can't go on or he did, he thought this can't go on this stacks of books and papers to get away, to get away I'd been in Corinth all those years before when all this started these books and notes and papers piled in front of me I'd go back, I'd go back, pack it all up and go back to Corinth, get a fresh start where it all began, see myself running through the streets went to Sparta, went to Pylos see myself at some sidewalk cafe making a note, reading all the time in the world sitting here sitting here reading and here it is! Here he is yes, going back to Palma to work, sees himself in Palma running through the street he can't even stand up and walk across the room he's done it again! My idea, my life, my work stolen it before I can get it down on paper it's the, no. No! No it's the, not Palma not Corinth not even the, no what's lost what's gone what's shouting in the streets is that youth when everything's possible good God that's what's gone forever. Young you're a child, get sick get well, get chicken pox get mumps get pneumonia pull the shades take your medicine and get well, get old and there's your pneumonia waiting round the corner the last best friend where the, damn. Bleeding again here, spill this water and that's the end, notes clippings books in one sodden heap better to bleed to death if this is the only reason not to, this work of mine trying to explain this other it's not Golyadkin no, it's not his doppelgänger who's gone with his bed in the morning when Petrushka brings in tea and explains that his master is not at home, shouting You idiot! I'm your master, Petrushka! and the "other one," Petrushka finally blurts out, the "other one" left hours ago it's not like that, this doppelgänger of Golyadkin's I've never even seen my, seen this plagiarist because I am the other one it's exactly the opposite, I am the other I just said that didn't I? It's exactly the opposite, sit here chatting like Seneca cutting his veins in the bath minute I stand up I am the other, we're not these Golyadkins we're not doppelgängers, it's either/or, it's all-or-none, it's this whole binary digitized pattern of holes punched in those millions of dusty piano rolls why I've got to find Dodds in these piles somewhere here while I'm thinking clearly, you see? Talks about the detachable self that can be withdrawn from the body, some kind of religious community Pythagoras set up with the idea of lives to come, and these dangerous demons with lives and energies of their own according to Homer was it? That aren't really part of yourself since you can't control them but they can force you to do things you wouldn't do otherwise before we get to the belly-talkers you hear about from Aristophanes and Plato they, good God sitting here alone in a room like something washed up from the ocean to have somebody, to have something to talk to! This second voice inside them they had conversations with and predicted the future in hoarse belly-voices and and, names? did they have names? Hello? Call him, hello Strabo? Call him Strabo, hello? You there? Rrrrrrr. Damn. Talk to me, tell me what the, you hear me? Maybe only speaks Greek, song and dance man, tum tum ti tum, tum tum ti hey! Predict the future for me then, hear me? This surgery, I have to know, foretell the future for me, have this surgery or these chemicals doing the same thing put me out of business? Strip the romantic veil off the naked animal's only, only, good God what am I doing talking to a, this detachable self, can't control it, it's not my fault makes you do things you wouldn't stop. Stop. Got to stop and go back make a fresh start when I find what I was looking for in this mess point is the first thing, point is to avoid stress get me, get my breath and avoid stress, newspapers tangled up in the sheets here reading the obituaries there are people dying I've never even heard of, haven't had a drink for seven years. Problem with Plato, what are the soft and drinking harmonies? Softness indolence drunkenness are unbecoming always giving you a rap across the knuckles looking for moral improvement the first thing, point is the first thing is to avoid stress what those Ionian and Lydian harmonies are for, help you avoid stress, avoid stress, avoi, no, no stop right here. Minute you're looking for something, doing something for pleasure he raps your knuckles banished the Lydian the Ionian, the rhythm, the instrument, goes right down the list. The harp and the lyre but only simple versions no fancy corners or complex scales must be in this pile, got to find Dodds on the Corybantes under here careful, carefully avoid stress worse than all the stringed instruments put together, isn't flute playing an art that seeks only pleasure? Out! Banished from his Republic and a little lecture there on good citizenship at the end of the Crito when Socrates says the sound of the flute humming in his ears he can't hear anything else now, now, ease it out I think I've got it don't, oh my God! Who, my God! Who would have put a glass of water back there! All over these newspapers these Japanese staples down my leg and books, papers where, can't stand up can't, get my breath can't, avoid, yes avoid stress but, oh my God. Sit here talking to these detachable selves bellytalkers kangaroos, thinking someone else's thoughts deadened out of existence and I'm the other, I am the other, sit here talking to automatons the Turkish lady in four languages Vaucanson's flute player like Galen's patient haunted by hallucinatory flutists he heard and saw day and night and another one Dodds mentions panics when a flute is played at a party but that's not the, that's the, not what Dodds calls an old Pythagorean catechism, "Pleasure" it says. "Pleasure is in all circumstances bad; for we came here to be punished and we ought to be punished" it's all, pictures the body as the soul's prison where the gods keep it locked up till it's purged of guilt, purgatorio! Madness, it's all madness, wanted to break out of this prison I, look at it, look at me, skin like tissue paper blotches that blossom daily blood spilled a week ago and this damned armoured leg, lungs shot and what's going on down below's nobody's business can't see across the room the whole thing's wreckage, top to bottom, a prison like this one break out of it like blowing out a candle I, I can't no I, I can't. Purgatory it's all purgatory beginning to end, catharsis right from the start. Flutes and kettledrums! Orgiastic music dancing people out of their minds talk about treating anxiety states, talk about avoiding stress about diagnosing madness in these Corybantic rituals out there banging away different tunes till they hit the one that belongs to the god who's possessing the patient the only one in this pandemonium he responds to, finds which god's tormenting him and pays him off sounds like the waterfront, sounds like buying indulgences pick your saint intercedes with Mary intercedes with Jesus intercedes with God knows what's all this guilt, original sin like a plague down the ages one heresy after another mortifying the body wait around long enough and it will do it for you, pushpin or poetry and here comes Mary Baker Eddy to say the whole thing's a mistake, an egregious pululating error and here's your sample wet right down to my God, my God, my God! I can't, see what's next foretell the future where every prospect pleases and only mine is, is like a long corridor doors opening off it closing off it fresh start go to one door closes when I get to it run to the next one and no! No here's my mail, soaking wet never even opened it spread it out to dry with the, what's this. What in God's name is this doing here, deeds to the properties land surveys title insurance, supposed to be in my safe how did it get here mixed up with my notes books papers what I came here to work on, my whole idea wasn't it? Get down to work fresh start don't let other things interfere avoid stress doors closing settle in, spread out like a prison like a tomb where the bed's the catafalque made by God the bedmaker in the last book of The Republic, talk about avoiding stress. Three kinds of beds God made one of them, if he'd made two a third one would have appeared behind them, the real bed not a particular bed, that's the carpenter, and then the painter imitating what they've made, good enough to fool children or the simple-minded out there waiting to be entertained you see I've got to explain all this because I don't, we don't know how much time there is and I have to work on the, to finish this work of mine while I, get it all sorted and organized before everything collapses and it's all swallowed up by lawyers and taxes like everything else because that's what it's about the collapse of everything of, of, I can't even go into it you see that's what I have to go into before all my ideas are stolen before I get them written down before my work is distorted misunderstood turned into a cartoon and, towel here in this mess somewhere sheet's cold and wet dry my leg before I start to rust, back of my hand all these little criss-crosses looks like broiled bluefish but, a little music. Music, that's really where it all starts and ends next time I see a human being I'll ask for a little music here not just for pleasure no, look for those notes on Nietzsche's Apollinian measured beauty in this heap somewhere but that's not what it's about no, it's this detachable self or soul being tormented in Hades or this guilt Empedocles gets from Pythagoras' school of recollection, training your memory to recollect sins and sufferings of your previous life in his terrifying catechism we came here to be punished and we ought to be punished, because good God! You find it wherever you look, the body as a prison and there's the rabbinical student dying of love for a woman engaged to somebody else so his spirit inhabits her body, slips in when she's asleep and her body's unoccupied and the rabbi comes in to exorcise this dybbuk, who may be having a grand time in there. This guilt, guilt, guilt step in it wherever you go in this pile somewhere, what was I looking for, these pages on Tolstoy no I put those under here with some broken, with this training your mind to recollect sins in a previous life to these cases today of recovered memory, same thing isn't it? Satanism and cannibalism and rape under the guidance of your psychotherapist, abuse and abortions and alien abductions with the help of your church counselor and these vivid fake memories of satanic cults where they practiced cannibalism and the poor woman is told to bring the meat in and they'll get it analyzed for human protein but I mean where did this Satan come from in the first place? Read them the script the crazier the better when the angel bursts in on this madman banished to a cave in the Aegean, saying with the voice of a trumpet What thou seest, write in a book, and goes on to dictate a scenario breathing fire and earthquake, the stars falling, the sun turning black and the sea turning to blood in that overwhelming vision of total insanity called the Revelation of St. John the Divine nearer to thee, dear God! Nearer to thee, and what do you say of the choral art and of dithyrambic poetry? Invented to give pleasure to the multitude aren't they? Talk about avoiding stress little cup here somewhere with pills in it, my head is splitting, just stop shivering, if I can just stop shivering, find a pencil here and get back to work if I can just stop shivering, now where was I, where was that. Flutes and kettledrums in the Corybantic and Dionysiac cures for phobias and anxiety breaking down and weeping, hearts beating like like, like the kettledrums dancing out of their minds in their morbid mental no, no it's getting too close can't dance can't even stand up that's the other can't, can't breathe just, just try to, put these back in this pile try to, to avoid stress get my breath and get back to work here's the voice of the mob the steam calliope getting closer hear it two miles away and the, wait. Wait yes here it is, what I was looking for not even 1910 yet, 1905, 1900 the automatic piano roll changer plays six five-tune rolls, look at it! Almost eight feet high weighs 1500 pounds the Wurlitzer

Orchestra piano with mandolin attachment, 38 violin pipes, 36 flute pipes, set of orchestra bells bass and snare drums and a triangle as though Plato had written the prescription for this pandemonium yes, yes his comments on the back here, banishing the imitative arts and the products of the imitative arts and the pantomimic artist who can imitate anything, "He will attempt to represent the roll of thunder, the noise of wind and hail, or the creaking of wheels, and pulleys, and the various sounds of flutes, pipes, trumpets, and all sorts of instruments: he will bark like a dog, bleat like a sheep, or crow like a," a sheep? Bleat like a lamb what was her name, that first animal cloned from a cell taken from an adult yes banishing the products of the imitative arts before we start to clone people? Not for me says a scientist who invents the techniques, to say how we should use them and goodbye Hiroshima, right here in the paper somewhere, if one of my relatives got cancer I'd clone him says another, use the clone to donate bone marrow to save the life of the, the body as a prison where we came here to be punished and we ought to be punished no we, pantomimics who can imitate anything got to stop here, it's, it's madness it's all madness thank God I'm not living now, get a fresh start in this pile where I put that diagram of this network of computers developing mutations that mimic natural selection and evolution all looked two dimensional so if you looked at them sideways you couldn't see them at all but that's, get a fresh start avoid stress get back to the, this pile here yes music haven't even looked through yet but, good God look. Look at this one! After eight years of constant labour it says here and this is in 1906 yes thank God I'm not living today. A refined musical attraction operated by electricity with nickel-in-the-slot attachment the Wurlitzer Harp look at it! Six feet six about Frankenstein's mimic's height, seven hundred fifty dollars with one perforated music roll, the harp is in full view covered by glass offering the opportunity watching the fingers (almost human) pick the strings like those, those tiny felt-tipped wooden fingers almost human, playing the lyre at festivals for pleasure? Remember Meles the harp player? No chance of him performing for the good of his hearers was there? Or even for their pleasure he was so bad, but harp playing was invented for the sake of pleasure wasn't it? So finally all of it's banished but the shepherd's pipe in the country and the lyre and the harp permitted in the city, extra rolls seven fifty and you can put in six nickels at once and get six tunes without getting to your feet again can't even feel my left one numb from the knee down if, if I can just stop shivering top to bottom the whole thing's wreckage except the heart, heart and arteries clean as whistles means the damn things will keep the prison going to enjoy every torment left, bad heart could take you out suddenly like Ambrose Bierce said, It beats old age, disease, and falling down the cellar steps find the pencil, I had a pencil get back to work's the only refuge but where was I? Clones and products of the imitative arts the pantomimics didn't know whether what they were cloning was good or bad, they wait, get this wet blanket off me here's a pill, prednisone oxycodone God knows what take it anyway my head's splitting, falls right into line doesn't it, collapse of authenticity collapse of religion collapse of values what Huizinga called one of the most important phases in the history of civilization, and Walter Benjamin picks it up in his Art in the Age of Mechanical Reproduction in this heap somewhere, the authentic work of art is based in ritual he says, and wait Mr. Benjamin, got to get in there the romantic mid-eighteenth century aesthetic pleasure in the worship of art was the privilege of the few. I was saying, Mr. Huizinga, that the authentic work of art had its base in ritual, and mass reproduction freed it from this parasitical dependence. Ah, quite so Mr. Benjamin quite so, turn of the century religion was losing its steam and art came in as its substitute would you say? Absolutely Mr. Huizinga, and I'd add that this massive technical reproduction of works of art could be manipulated, changed the way the masses looked at art and manipulated them. Inadvertently Mr. Benjamin, you might say that art now became public property, for the simply educated Mona Lisa and the Last Supper became calendar art to hang over the kitchen sink. Absolutely Mr. Huizinga, Paul Valéry saw it coming, visual and auditory images brought into homes from far away like water gas and electricity and finally, God help us all, the television. Positively Mr. Benjamin, with mechanization, advertising artworks made directly for a market what America's all about. Always has been, Mr. Huizinga. Always has been, Mr. Benjamin. Everything becomes an item of commerce and the market names the price. And the price becomes the criterion for everything. Absolutely Mr. Huizinga! Authenticity's wiped out when the uniqueness of every reality is overcome by the acceptance of its reproduction, so art is designed for its reproducibility. Give them the choice, Mr. Benjamin, and the mass will always choose the fake. Choose the fake, Mr. Huizinga! Authenticity's wiped out, it's wiped out Mr. Benjamin. Wiped out, Mr. Huizinga. Choose the fake, Mr. Benjamin. Absolutely, Mr. Huizinga! Positively Mr. Benjamowww! Good God! a way to find a sharp pencil just sit still avoid stress stop singing what, anybody heard me they'd think I was losing my, that I'd lost it yes maybe I have but I've got to get back to the products of the imitative arts and the pantomimics all falls right into line, bark like a dog bleat like a Little Lamb, who made thee? Dost thou know who made thee? Gave thee such a tender voice, making all the vales rejoice? Little Lamb, who made thee? Dost thou know who made thee? Little Lamb, I'll tell thee, Little Lamb, I'll tell thee: Doctor Wilmut made thee, Doctor Ian Wilmut cloned thee outside Edinburgh, Scotland, a product of the imitative arts that Plato banished find a piece of paper got to get this down, you see? Cloned like slaves by the pantomimics who could imitate anything like, yes like the black slaves bred in Virginia when Eli Whitney's cotton gin revolutionized the world markets for American cotton, people making millions, the African slave trade forbidden, illegal, over and done, so breeding slaves to cultivate the cotton turned Virginia into an immense breeding farm says Henry Adams' sharper brother exporting 40,000 blacks a year to the southern states' plantations where the market set the price piece of paper two whole heaps of it but they're all no wait, letter here almost dry from those eye test doctors about clearing up this bleary vision with the predni, what in the, prednisone? Not the prednisone it says, you have developed cataracts and should make appointments for the operations necessary to correct this condition as promptly as good God! Operations? They think I'm a, same thing it's the same thing it's the same damn damn thing breeding slaves to be reproduced where the market sets the price where slavery wouldn't be abolished George Washington said till it ceased to pay, being cloned to serve as bone banks letter in one of these heaps somewhere when I had a car asking if I'd like to be an organ eye and tissue donor see their faces when they open this package! Over fifty thousand out there waiting for these organ transplants, the first interchangeable parts made for guns by this same Eli Whitney two hundred years ago getting a little bit mixed up here why I've got to write this down before it's lost, before it's stolen, just to get the sequence right, what follows what, post hoc ergo this game you can't win because that's not why you play it trying to cultivate this whole swamp of chaos and chance, of paradox and perversity to wipe out the whole idea of cause and effect and, and, get my breath before I lose the, these belly-talkers and detached selves bred and cloned to be reproduced because that's the heart of it, where the individual is lost, the unique is lost, where authenticity is lost not just authenticity but the whole concept of authenticity, that love for the beautiful creation before it's created that that, it was Chesterton wasn't it? That natural merging of created life in this creation in love that transcends it, a celebration of the love that created it they called agapē, that love feast in the early church, yes. That's what's lost, what you don't find in these products of the imitative arts that are made for reproduction on a grand scale got to find some paper, piece of blank paper I've finally got the pencil now, now. Chance to straighten something out here's Friedrich's book where's the other one, getting them mixed up I can mark the passages and find who said what, find Glenn Gould, can't do better than Friedrich's biography it's stunning, a marvelous writer journalist and a prodigy, a piano prodigy himself, thousands of notes but which one? Spent six weeks making notes and sketches about Glenn that could be either one of them, finally decided they got in the way of what he was writing so he destroyed them all but that sounds like Wertheimer destroying his thousands of notes before he hanged himself, be the best or not at all that's Horowitz, a lot of malice and envy for Horowitz could be both of them, either of them either book but why, envy for Horowitz's brilliance or for his applause because Gould said he detested appearing before an audience and detested their applause didn't he? Because it's easy to let the piano become your enemy because it symbolizes the terror of the performance, if I hadn't met Gould I wouldn't have given up the piano, no more piano! I said. Absolutely no artist! The Goldberg Variations composed to help get an insomniac through the night, pleasure in all circumstances is bad says Pythagoras composed to delight the soul and they killed Wertheimer because we came here to be punished and we ought to be punished getting a little mixed up here by these detachable selves and demons making you do things you wouldn't when Glenn got so carried away performing a Bach concerto he cut his thumb on the keys in his exuberant finale? Then would he have said he wanted to become the piano? That he wanted to be the Steinway because he hated the idea of being between Bach and the Steinway because if he could be the Steinway he wouldn't need Glenn Gould he'd be the other. He'd be the Steinway and Glenn in one like the kangaroo he'd be the other! He'd be in control, he'd be in total control with his splicing and editing and altering pitch what he called creative cheating for the perfect performance with an arching melodic line that couldn't be mechanically imitated but it could be it was that's what all this is to, damn. Got it all there somewhere can't find the other book got the pencil didn't have time to write it down and it's more confused than ever but that's what it's all about that's the heart of it all can't lose it, can't lose it now because I had it wrong good thing I didn't write it down all that business of authenticity and the perfect performance what did I just say, the melodic line that couldn't be mechanically imitated because it was yes in Germany yes where else? Family named Welte in Freiburg with the reproducing piano, the Welte-Mignon that didn't just record the notes but more perforations that actually reproduced all the shadings and subtleties of the artist, the unique performances of their own work by Debussy and Grieg, Rachmaninoff George Gershwin and the greatest pianists, Paderewski and God knows who, don't you see? These Welte, Duo-Art Pianolas, Ampico all over the place what they'd done was to make the transient permanent, given the fleeting nature of music of great performances of great music a permanence that's the heart of authenticity, that preserved the whole concept of authenticity stood Leonardo da Vinci on his ear holding painting an art superior to music because of music's evanescent quality can't lose it no, don't have to write it down I can't forget it, it's beautiful, simple and beautiful like discovering space is curved good God, just the sheer simplicity of it the, where Occam's razor looked on beauty bare got to write it down before it gets lost, before it gets stolen before I have a chance to write it down like everything else because if Gould hated the idea of being between Bach and the Steinway if he could be the Steinway he wouldn't need Glenn Gould when Welte's reproducing apparatus put Debussy into the piano then you wouldn't need Debussy. You wouldn't need Grieg you wouldn't need Gershwin or Paderewski or any of them because you'd have their authenticity and the whole concept of authenticity preserved, the music itself and the fleeting performance brought together forever, given permanence that's the heart of authenticity like the, there must be some law of physics for this, for the or maybe it's, maybe I've discovered one. No more piano! Absolutely no artist, no more so-called legendary performances oh my grandmother heard Paganini, absolutely fabulous they said he was in league with the devil yes one of these dangerous demons with lives and energies of their own you can't control that can force you to do things you wouldn't otherwise, or Gottschalk? Louis Moreau Gottschalk? A brilliant stunning pianist, Chopin said he was, so did Liszt, so did Berlioz, that's the performer we'll never hear, but the composer? The music he wrote? It's so bad, honky-tonk and bouncy what he'd done, listen. Just like my plagiarist writing my ideas before I had them, he wrote music for the worst nickel-in-the-slot player piano fifty years before the player was invented. Pushpin or poetry it's the quantity of pleasure in these enormous markets of the non-musical and the half-musical, these chance persons with no true sense of musical values because they don't hear, they simply have no ear for music they don't know pianissimo from sforzando, diminuendos from crescendos and those elegant gradations that distinguish the performance of one artist from another on these reproducing piano rolls went for ten, fifteen dollars for the Welte-Mignon they couldn't dream of paying for these unique subtleties they simply couldn't hear, as though their ears were closed against the racket of American industrial strife everywhere like my left ear was closed from grinding my teeth at night from stress, yes. Yes avoid stress, good God to go through that again maybe I still do. Maybe I still grind my teeth at night no way to know because I'm asleep? Nobody to hear me maybe it's closed now and I don't even know it because there's nothing to hear if I, no wait, wait if I hold that glass against it and tap it with the where is the pencil, just stop shivering get this wet sheet over the, move my leg so numb I don't even know where it is good God to go through that again with the hockey mouthguard twelve seconds in boiling water two seconds in cold put it in your mouth to mould it doesn't really matter if my left ear is closed though does it if there's nothing to hear anyhow get my mind off it, avoid stress just get my mind back on the, on what it was on turn of the century mob coming in from southern Europe meant that collective poor Roman Catholic audience for the pantomimic's products of the imitative arts produced to be reproduced just like themselves where the priest's the pandomimic and the gap gets wider, just look back at the great 1890 census that Hollerith put together now there's the beginning. There was the beginning of key-sort and punched cards and IBM and NCR and the whole driven world we've inherited from some rinky-dink piano roll widening the gap when Aeolian finally got into the reproducing piano act with their Duo-Art Pianola piano right before the war, they'd put one into a Steinway, for the pleasure of Plato's best educated elite and the unique great artist whose use of the sostenuto and soft pedals and his tempo phrasing and attack they pretended they could hear giving demonstrations and testimonials for Welte and Aeolian and Ampico and Angelus and Apollo, because these things ran four or five thousand dollars even before they started the wood carving on the case like Tom Mix in the manner of the Spanish Renaissance to match his house or the gilded garlands and decorations on the old ivory enamel case for the juvenile movie star Jackie Coogan or Rudolph Valentino's Angelus they're all here I just saw it, where's the list royalty right down the line I just yes, Dowager Empress of China letter here from Prince Ch'ing gets the jump on them all with her Apollo piano player back in 1906 goes right on to something I wrote in the margin what's the last ⅛" 51 100/thndth sec this my writing? Must be, shaky uncertain like every wrong decision I've ever made never made any other kind, never came through for anybody, why I end up here with a hopeless project like this one conversations with these detachable selves and belly-talkers get back to the slurred letters in dght can't even read it shows character that's what's at the heart of the whole thing, lack of character see right here where money my ideas of money, my whole view of money has warped my entire life and the, all the, stress yes avoid stress widening the gap between Freud's nickel and dime trash and Plato's wealthy educated elite with these reproducing pianos in the Élysée Palace in Paris and Queen Mary in London, ex-King Ferdinand of Bulgaria, the Sultan of Turkey, the Khedive of Egypt, the Shah of Persia and the King of Siam, Mussolini in Rome, the Dowager Queen of Italy, the Duchess of Argyll and Her Late Majesty the Empress Alexandra Feodorovna of Russia direct line back to Marie Antoinette's gold canary and that mob at the Bastille but here the widening gap was money and democracy, between the Ampico in Vincent Astor's music room and six Autopianos on the battleship USS Delaware, between Helen Keller in the forest when the tree falls and the, no, no wait. Wait, this whole discovery I just made yes that's what this is, this scribble in the margin it's the technology! good God the technology! A hundred years ago this recording instrument that measured the time it took the hammer on the last eighth of an inch before it strikes the string for exact loudness, to fifty-one hundred-thousandths of a second! It's the whole thing! It's the proof of the whole thing, of my whole idea my whole thesis entertainment the parent of technology I should, I could write and publish a paper separate from this big project, combine this with authenticity preserved in the music itself and the fleeting performance by its finest interpreter or the composer himself like Grieg playing his dreadful Wedding March piece of paper here somewhere get it all written down before somebody steals it, of course if I write it down that's almost an invitation to steal it, mail all over the place here drying out just something to write on because this is the heart of it right back to the start, you see? Back to Vaucanson's flutist gives us Jacquard's loom back to pleasure that's bad in all circumstances and Pythagoras' terrible catechism sit here wet as a hen suddenly see the underside of my arm royal purple didn't even have to bang it, must have just pressed my weight on it got to get some, get my breath avoid stress just get my mind off the, back on the pantomimics and clones and mechanization of everything in sight, entertainment and the binary system and all-or-none computer where its technology came from in the first place, don't really give one damn for it, for any of it, like this dangerous demon you can't control not really part of you but can force you to do things you, head's splitting grinding my teeth if anybody heard me they'd think I was losing my, that I've lost it yes maybe I have why I've got to get back to the, to things you can weigh and count and measure the technology good God yes the technology! A hundred years ago measuring the time it took the hammer on the last eighth of an inch of tape down to fifty-one hundred-thousandths of a second? Not for some great breakthrough in medical science no, not for advanced weapons design or aero, for aerodynamics no, for entertainment, for pleasure in its highest form for music to entertain Plato's educated elite, widening the gap yes, between Huizinga's eighteenth century, when aesthetic pleasure in the worship of art was the privilege of the few, and this democracy of every man his own artist where we are today, this democracy of Plato's chance persons and having art without the artist because he's a threat, because the creative artist has to be a threat so he's swamped by the performer by the, by the pantomimic by the imitative who is not a threat see it right here in the, right here in Jung yes from the depths of his Swiss hypocrisy he's an inveterate democrat he says but nature is aristocratic, that it's elitist and so is he, Quod licet Jovi he quotes, non licet bovi draws the line right there doesn't he? An unpleasant but eternal truth he called it what's so damned unpleasant about that? Eternal truth that's what it's all about isn't it? The poet, the artist set apart from the common herd by some inner illumination that Plato thought was, because that's not even Plato no it's Dodds damn it where's Dodds? Had it right here didn't I? I know I brought it, brought some Flaubert some Nietzsche Huysmans Heidegger some Tolstoy even brought Friedrich and The Physics of Baseball but, didn't I bring it? Because it was Democritus, right there in Dodds it was Democritus saying the finest poems were composed with "inspiration and a holy breath" I remember that phrase, inspiration and the holy breath that sets us apart from reason and above reason, some inner revelation, some inner ecstasy even some abnormal mental state why they're out to eliminate us, why they'd say I'm afraid of the death of the elite because it means the death of me of course I can't really blame them, I've been wrong about everything in my life it's all been fraud and fiction, let everybody down except my daughters maybe I can still rescue them, not their fault is it? Fact that I'm forgotten that I'm left on the shelf with the dead white guys in the academic curriculum that my prizes are forgotten because today everybody's giving prizes for that supine herd out there waiting to be entertained, try to educate them did they buy those "Educator" piano rolls teach them to play with their hands no, went right on discovering their unsuspected talent playing with their feet here's Flaubert yes, "The entire dream of democracy" he says, "is to raise the proletariat to the level of bourgeois stupidity." You want the essence of elitism there he was, his idea of art that "the artist must no more appear in his work than God does in nature, that the artist must manage to make posterity believe that he never existed" good God, the rate things change a generation lasts about four days what posterity? Everywhere present and nowhere visible leads him right into the embrace of the death of the author whose intentions have no connection with the meaning of the text which is indeterminate anyway, a multidimensional space where the modern scriptor is born with this, this detachable self this second voice inside predicting the future in its hoarse belly-voice, Strabo? You hear me? Strip the romantic veil off the naked animal's only purpose perpetuating the species the race the tribe the family for everybody else sex is for pleasure like the flute, pushpin or poetry "the most intense pleasure of which man is capable" says my golden Sigi, seek pleasure avoid not a clue what they're being used for even that they're being used till the roof falls in, doctors lawyers abortions adulteries thimble theatre learned nothing forgotten nothing go right back and do it all again. "My one impulse is to work and forget" says Tolstoy "but forget what. There's nothing to forget" and then? here's the scrap, "I shall write no more fiction," he's about thirty, "people are weeping, dying, marrying, and I should sit down and write books telling 'how she loved him'? It's shameful!" And where else yes here, "reading bad books helps me to detect my own faults more than good ones. Good books reduce me to despair" maybe where the idea for this whole absurd project of mine here came from this fear of failure, the technology the artist created being used to eliminate him and the piano, the player piano and its offspring the computer barricades against this fear of chance, of probability and indeterminacy that's so American, this fear this stigma of failure which separates the crowd from the elite when Flaubert writes to George Sand "I believe that the crowd, the mass, the herd, will always be detestable. Nothing is important save a small group of minds, ever the same, which pass on the torch" try to sit up straight here stopped shivering and dry out mind's clear as a bell, everything falling right into place get it all down before the belly-talkers come back with the death of the author, the artist's solitary enterprise with the individual reader Hawthorne talked about horrified at success with the public taste, with the crowd meant you must have sold out, send the author of The Marble Faun out on a book tour? Out giving readings from The Blithedale Romance to entertain this gaping clutch of pleasure seeking chance persons, this enormous market of the non-literate and half-literate devouring the poets who compose to please the bad taste of their reviewers end up instructing one another, what this glorious democracy in the arts is all about isn't it? Get up there and perform with what Hawthorne called "that damned mob of scribbling women," even Poe with his mechanized genius for forcing order on chaos scorning the public and thirsting for fame, and Melville, good God Melville? Begins Moby Dick wants everybody to read it finishes daring them to, has to borrow money to write it because Harper's won't give him an advance, they publish it and he still owes them a hundred and forty-five dollars and eighty-three cents never forget that figure, "dollars damn me!" he tells Hawthorne, writes that terrible Pierre you can't get thirty pages into hates feeling he must take his readers where they expect to go, talk about elitism about setting yourself apart from the common herd beyond reason above reason on the shelf with the dead white guys ends up in the Custom House at four dollars a day reduced to a nonperson, to herd anonymity humiliated castrated eliminated as a threat that's what it's all about that's what I have to explain. Of course you can't really explain anything to anybody that's why all we hear are explanations of these explanations get right back to Wiener with his more complicated the message the more chance for error so stay with the June moon cliché on the fifty cent piano roll what this deification of democracy's all about, what this tyranny of the majority that Mill got from de Tocqueville's all about that made him famous, Mill never had an idea of his own in his life till that winter he got seriously tormented he said that the range of musical combinations might be exhausted. Five tones and two semitones in an octave you can put together in a limited number of ways only a few are beautiful and must have already been used up no more Mozart, no more Weber, like the head of the U.S. Patent Office resigning in 1875 because he thought everything that could be invented had been invented in that frenzy of invention flooding America only really began a year later with the yes with, the player piano always come back to it, all roads lead to Rome try to explain anything always come back to it, why this ought to be subsidized this work of mine look at it. Look at this mess, this bed this empty room these medicines cost of these medicines headache is gone clear as a bell must be these medicines whole thing government supported like it ought to be problem is you have to be wiped out. Have to be reduced to this herd anonymity, humiliated and eliminated as an artist like Melville got a nickel left they'll make you spend it go to work in the Custom House to survive as a citizen you have to become a nonperson, own one square foot of property means you're still self-sufficient because your property's who you are that's what America what the West is all about what it's always been about what I'm trying to explain here. Can't really explain anything to anybody no but if we could if you could just explain it to yourself and, and wait, damn! Should have brought those deeds, land surveys, title insurance tax records get the properties divided and cleared up and settled on my daughters before it's all swallowed by lawyers and taxes and I'm drawn and quartered by the government supposed to be helping me out backing me up all I've paid in taxes years and years of taxes become propertyless now divide everything three ways one for each daughter and we all benefit, let them worry about the upkeep repairs rents administering the properties and I spend a third of the year with each of them, get on with my work they look out for me and I'm allowed to show my generosity and they have the opportunity to show their love for me. Give them my money now give them all my cash securities God knows what they'd pay taxes on it and I'd have to wait thirty-two months for the government to come through but they'd probably just pay the taxes make sure they get the money now and we're all left out in the cold, don't even know what it all comes to statements probably right here in this heap of wet mail but they're my only refuge. Loss, loss all just loss wherever you look, only refuge I've got left for my, for what's left of my memory my discovery what I thought was my, would be sort of my vest pocket immortality and my, yes for my generosity and dignity, none of it left anyplace else I just took off in the wrong directions. Wrong about everything all so long ago, about everybody especially friends, thought we were all friends so full of who I thought I was some buffoon all two dimensional some cartoon minute I turned sideways they couldn't see me at all, left on the shelf forgotten work forgotten my prizes forgotten when a prize still meant something now everybody out there giving prizes to each other not even for winners no we're all just props for the ones who give the prizes, pantomimics imitation entertainment for this supine half-literate and non-literate crowd out there have to be read to it's all, good God why did we learn to read in the first place? You read to three year olds, get up and give a reading give a performance none of that fierce authenticity of Hawthorne between the writer and the reader, between the reader and the page what it's all about, that solitary enterprise between him and the individual reader yes, the one who comes after you with an ax in the middle of the night or Melville's grotesque hero who wants to be a popular novelist must have written Pierre out of revenge, only revenge the mob has on them both is to go to the movies, thirty fifty a hundred million dollars against a hundred forty-five dollars and eighty-three cents, the final great stupefying collective. No more illusion of taking part, of discovering your unsuspected talent when the biggest thrill in music was playing it yourself, your own participation that roused your emotions most no, no. The ultimate collective, the herd numbed and silenced agape at blood sex and guns blowing each other to pieces only participation you get's maybe kids who see it come to school next morning and mow down their classmates no more elitism no more elite no wherever you turn just the spread of the crowd with its, what did he call it, what Huizinga called its insatiable thirst for trivial recreation and crude sensationalism, the mass of the mediocre widening the gap the popularity of a work is the measure of its mediocrity says Melville no news there is there? The masses invading the province of the writer says Walter Benjamin a hundred years later, by now the fences are down there's no province left, on the shelf with the dead white guys you want the real gap, a look from the heights down on the mass of men who aren't worth anything in the first place, that there's a greater gap between some men and others than between these others and the animal kingdom yes that was Nietzsche before they twisted him all out of shape and the whole, get my breath here yes avoid stress try to get the, get my leg here makes him sound like what little my golden Sigi found any good about those human beings telling Reverend Oskar Pfister in his experience most of them are trash coming one way and Tolstoy the other with his duty to these scraps, just had them these scraps of Tolstoy under the wait, wait been looking for this yes that shot of mitoxantrone side effects may cause shortness of breath, lower back pain, swelling feet and lower legs good God from whom all bless- ings flow but which ones? No discolouration at the site here where the needle went into the vein, unusual bruising or bleeding what do they call unusual? Other arm's already purple this one blossoming like a flower garden, red eyes yellow eyes whites of the eyes turn blue no way to see them any more than hearing grinding my teeth if there's nothing to hear, blood on the no it's not the blood on the shirt here it's the shirt yes doesn't look like my shirt was a broadcloth Egyptian cotton broadcloth this looks like a coarse muslin no collar on it either is there? Can't see clearly no mirror on the wall over there a long time ago, when we rented this place to an actress one summer, and that purple velour chair there in the corner with the long tear down the cushion where her dog, she had a German shepherd dog where it tore a streak down the cushion too good a story to have it repaired but the, but I, not seeing too well get a little disoriented sometimes but this room is, when we rented out the whole place here that year but it's not the change no but how fast the changes come now, not even the weeks the years but how many different lives you've lived, first step that counts yes I always took the wrong one like being five, ten, twenty different people wouldn't know each other if they met in the street wouldn't even say hello, you see? No. No it doesn't matter does it because you don't believe me so it doesn't really matter, lies and falsehood wherever you look why I brought along Huysmans with his party waited on by these stunning naked black women and his symphony of liqueurs, his symphony of flowers and the flowers that look fake, that everything is fake like the room like a ship with mechanical fish and that marvelous description of two new locomotives as women, the deliberate cultivation of the fake and the false in this French novel more than a century ago, À Rebours in 1884 even then an elitist gloss on a culture whose literature and art are being ruined by greed and the embrace of the mob, the what, the epiphany, the embodiment of mediocrity and everything repellent about it even then! and the source of this rot even then yes, America, no news there is there? Lies and falsehood bursting from the mob's mistrust of the elite wherever you looked, mistrust of the intellectual who Tolstoy called untrustworthy, useless and artificial nourished on books not experience who'd never fought in a war or plowed a field so their writings produced nothing but lies why you don't believe me because they're the common currency aren't they. Falsehood's the common currency and we're back where we started, not the pure unadulterated falsehood but what Plato calls the lie in words that's only sort of an imitation, a shadowy image that's useful sometimes when you're dealing with an enemy for instance that's all we do isn't it? Why Tolstoy says it's our duty to edify the masses, our vocation to edify mankind even for the ones who think you can teach without knowing anything since artists and poets teach unconsciously, that music, literature, painting all the arts are just a stew of nonsense and falsehood if the masses don't support them because where is it yes yes here. "Perhaps they don't understand and don't want to understand our literary language because it's not suited to them and they're in the process of inventing their own literature" Tolstoy wrote that, we must write what they want or not write at all, "we are thousands and they are millions" Tolstoy writes, obey the law of the greatest number talk about the tyranny of the majority here's Ezra Pound widening the gap to the degree the serious artist lets his audience's values shape his own vision, he lies, can't say Tolstoy wasn't serious can you? That our literary language isn't suited to his common herd of millions out there maybe they're inventing their own, been to the movies lately? Listened to their lyrics?! Man I mean like I've heard it you dumb asshole give this muhthrfuckr a blowjob every man his own artist in this democracy of the arts lined up Walt

Whitman singing his body electric didn't we? American classic Leaves of Grass he says the poet's merit is determined by the multitude good God, write what they want you'll end up with a Pulitzer Prize follow you right to the grave. Maybe won the Medal of Honor the George Cross even the Nobel but once you've been stigmatized with the ultimate seal of mediocrity your obit will read Pulitzer Prize Novelist Dies at whatever because they're not advertising the winner no. No, like this whole plague of prizes wherever you look, it's the prize givers promoting themselves, trying to rescue their thoroughly discredited profession of journalism. "The press is a school that serves to turn men into brutes," Flaubert writes to George Sand "because it relieves them from thinking." The prize winners? They're just props, cartoonists, sports writers, political pundits, front page photos the bloodier the better for that instant of fame wrap the fish in tomorrow, good God how many Pulitzer Prizes are there? Over fifteen hundred entries, fourteen categories for journalists because if you started your bondage there you're halfway home with that whole gang of sponsors, trustees, juries, God knows what who've survived that Slough of Despond and floated to the top. Just look at the next day's New York Times, page after page bulging with self-congratulation with seven more categories to leech on, music, what they call drama and of course books where the Grey Lady finally got it both ways with their journalist who reviews books, like the misty-eyed ingenue but destroys women writers and just for fairness crosses the gender line for an occasional assassination, give that lady a Pulitzer with oak leaf clusters! The books that are candidates are read by a jury whose decisions are passed up to the Olympian trustees with an eye to the multitude. We are thousands and they are millions, write the fiction they want or don't write at all, ruling out Pound's cry for the new, the challenging or what's labeled difficult, so when Gravity's Rainbow is being devoured by college youth everywhere and wins the National Book Award, its unanimous recommendation by the Pulitzer jury is overturned by the trustees for a double-talk spoof of academic vagaries by a bogus "Professor," to everyone's relief, and the author at peril escapes unblemished by the, no, no, no you can't depend on it. Step on more sensitive toes with a brilliant biography of William Randolph Hearst that's a sure bet for a serious Pulitzer jury's selection and, pow! The trustees, still held in mortmain by their mouldering Demiurge, look the book over and stumble on Pulitzer himself portrayed as tall and rail thin, a blind nervous wreck given to profane rages, jumping out of his skin at the sound of tearing paper, weeping and cursing on his infrequent visits to his newspaper office when he's not in the soundproof rooms of his New York house, in one of his far-flung mansions or aboard his oceangoing yacht Liberty, called a "journalist who made his money by pandering to the worst tastes of the prurient and the horror-loving" by this free-spending Harvard Lampoon prankster who's left fireworks and chamberpots behind for this cutthroat carnival of journalism, and who promptly follows suit to the letter. Hearst's Journal and Pulitzer's World, nothing they wouldn't do, accuse the other of and promptly improve upon in the name of circulation and even survival, bogus news and personal thievery, scraping the bottom for crime and sordid sensationalism to bring the stupidity level of the bourgeoisie down to the subliterate appetite of the proles. Bogus news? It was, who was it, it was Pasteur wasn't it in a happier context who observed that chance favours the prepared mind? And after all, all this bloodletting was going on just a century ago, when the US battleship Maine lay in

Havana harbour waiting on the unswerving punctuality of chance to seize upon the prepared mind of Hearst and change the course of empires, dragging his reluctant antagonist with him. Bogus news and we're right back with Plato's lie in words aren't we? Imitations, sort of shadowy images useful when you're dealing with an enemy whose name pursues its victims to the grave yes but, no but listen. Since all writing worth reading comes, like suicide, from outrage or revenge, there must still be a way to deal with some serious ideas here without risking this seal of Tolstoy edifying the masses, in this novel published by some nickel and dime southern university press. Talk about the classic contributions of Aristotle and Plato in the participatory democracy of ancient Athens in creating the sense of community, just scare them all away. Places like Athens and Laodicea might as well be on the moon, names like Leonidas sound like a zoo, look for Athens you read New Orleans, hide the great ideas someplace, disguise them, mask them and let them break out with a life of their own, a character who yes some simple name like Jones. His name's Jones, dark glasses spewing cigarette smoke answering an ad for a job as a porter in a honky-tonk nightclub, he's asked for a character reference. "A po-lice gimme a reference. He tell me I better get my ass gainfully employ" Jones says. "I ain exactly a character yet, but I can tell they gonna star that vagran no visible mean of support stuff on me. I thought maybe the Night of Joy like to help somebody become a member of the community, help keep a poor color boy outta jail. I keep the picket off, give the Night of Joy a good civil right ratin." Experience? The pay is twenty dollars a week. "Wha? Sweepin and moppin and all that nigger shit? Hey! No wonder the right man ain show up. Ooo-wee. Say, whatever happen to the minimal wage? The las person workin in here musta starve to death. Don worry. I come in regular, anything keep my ass away from a po-lice for a few hour. Where you keep them motherfuckin broom?" See what he's done? Isn't that glorious? Aristotle defining politics as the struggle between the rich and the poor hasn't changed a damn bit, has it? Maybe this sense of community they're talking about would be accomplished by widening the rights of citizenship to the poorest class? Remember this great cradle of participating democracy depends on slave labor, whose participation may not be that enthusiastic, and Plato sees that force alone won't ensure submission of the poor and lower classes, to make it work you've got to instill a sense of irremediable inferiority in the hearts and minds of these poor and lower classes, deny them these rights of citizenship and treat them like a different race? "She think cause I color I gonna rape her" Jones conjures of the woman sitting beside him on the bus. "She about to throw her grammaw ass out the window. Whoa! I ain gonna rape nobody. I gonna tell that po-lice I gainfully employ, keep him off my back, tell him I met up with a humanitaria payin me twenty dollar a week. He say, 'That fine, boy. I'm glad to see you straighten out.' And I say, 'Hey!' And he say, 'Now maybe you be becomin a member of the community.' And I say, 'Yeah, I got me a nigger job and nigger pay. Now I really a member of the community. Now I a real nigger. No vagran. Just nigger.' Whoa!" Good God, see what he's done? It's glorious. Are we what our mothers made us? His spends the next ten years breaking her neck to get it published and of course, it wins the Pulitzer Prize for fiction, it's the book bears the blemish in a last bow to journalism, "Whoa! That paper sure sending out plenny mothers taking pictures and axin me all about wha happen. Who say a color cat cain get his picture on the front page? Ooo-wee! Whoa! I gonna be the mos famous vagran in the city!" get you one way or the other, Book Award they give you ten thousand for biting the hands that feed you every minion in publishing at that black tie dinner at the Plaza must run them half a million just a, get my breath here yes avoid stress maybe try to get my leg over the side here and, just a shadowy image isn't it? Isn't all of it? Count Tolstoy pounding it to stray peasant girls in the wheat field drops in to haunt this elegant Europeanized weepy panicky no, no gets too close where are those Tolstoy scraps yes, getting too close following Turgenev everywhere with his piercing terrifying glare "enough to drive a man mad" Turgenev tells a friend "with a few vicious remarks" and he's in tears again, can't understand "this ridiculous affection for a wretched title of nobility" he's, you see? Can't, can't, gets too close being tormented like this by some monstrous, some detachable self, some dangerous demon not really part of you since you can't control it but can force you to do things you, can't let you get away from him follows Turgenev home like a dog can't, getting a little confused here getting my dates mixed up doesn't matter no, when Tolstoy was still much younger doesn't really matter because you don't believe me anyway just the shadowy image the imitation gets home shattered getting shaky, getting my breath here get my leg over the side staples are dry just to get the blood running get the, get my pencil get the mail's still wet yes he gets the mail, letter from Flaubert says he just wants to be around long enough to dump a few more buckets of merde on the heads of his countrymen, end of an elite end of an era of, whole leg down there numb and heavy as a, foot numb and heavy as a clubfoot or do they just look numb and heavy? Publishes Childe Harold he's famous a great hero great romantic hero scandals money horrors forced to sell his estate get out of England but why Greece? Maybe's just a metaphor but who's the metaphor? Byron for Greece fighting for freedom from the Turks or Greece for him, fighting for a fresh start, get rid of the fiction or be the fiction because he hated the idea of being between them if he could be the fiction he wouldn't need Byron, strip the romantic veil off the naked animal's only purpose being used to perpetuate the race sex with girls sex with boys not for pleasure no out of sheer despair sell the estate, go back to Greece make a fresh start because this place was a fiction when I bought it, put in that breakfront over there window frames rotting replaced them with casements sell the whole thing be-

cause this Other I bought it for was a fiction kangaroo and all the rest of it I can't, can't tell if I'm shivering or just have the shakes try to get upright here
my leg to, to avoid stress yes don't, don't don't try to
stand up if I fell I'd never get up again pack it all up
and get back to Corinth running through the streets,
sitting at that cafe table reading was that, that was
youth yes was that, was youth a fiction? No sweet
sauces, no fancy Sicilian cooking no Athenian sweets
no, girlfriend, allowed to have a Corinthian girlfriend? Certainly not! Pleasure deprives man of the
use of his faculties, any greater pleasure than sensual
love? No, nor a madder, true love is beauty and order
so no intemperance or madness allowed near our true
loving couple all of it fictions falsehoods lies, people
weeping, dying, marrying, and I should sit down
and write books telling "how she loved him"? says
Tolstoy, it's shameful! The ultimate fiction the mad-
dest of them all yes the most tyrannous because they
believe it kill for it, die for it, only you! Has to be the
most absurd, the most overwhelming fiction because
of the enormity of what it has to conceal till it's too
late yes, these illusions this fiction of love true love
mad love strip it all away and lay things bare get
the, get that towel I'm sweating I'm, even Wagner

preaching love but he punishes all of them, Sieg-
mund and Sieglinde, Siegfried and Brünnhilde burns
them up for giving in, from all the foreplay Huizinga
calls it just play, just imitation, over to the real
thing, the true lie good God, ever see Montecavallo
up there filling the stage? Good breeding stock but
she's a victim of the true lie, the one who's deceived
in the soul and she's punished for it, they all are, follows Hegel here they say where suffering's necessary
for self realization shades of the Pythagorean catechism two or three thousand years ago here to be
punished if I can, hold on to something sit up
straight and get the other leg over why they, why I
was put in this empty room no light, no air can't,
sweating as if I'm, if I'm frightened? Feeling everything's beginning to slide try to concentrate yes,
mind's as clear as it get myself oriented let it get myself oriented, Tolstoy says Pascal had a nail-studded
belt he'd lean against when some word of praise
pleased him good God! His powers are weakening he
says, his profession is dreadful, "writing corrupts the
soul" yes, we are thousands and they are millions
that's exactly why the shape of his work isn't up to
him, says Plato. That's the business of the state.
These poets and other artists must not show inde-

cency and intemperance so the first thing to be done is to censor writers of fiction or they'll corrupt the citizens growing up among images of moral deformity, because youth can't tell the difference between allegory and what's literal even in the great storytellers so it's that or be banished, show only the image of the good or be banished because, it's no, do you believe it? Because no, got to stop it's all coming to pieces like the, like the belly-talker talking to the belly-talker because there's no difference now between allegory and what's literal, let lyric verse in there and pleasure and pain rule the state, the soul can't be filled with variety and difference and dissimilarity and we're back in this swamp of paradox perversity, ambiguity, aporia back where we started, listen. Listen. This is the heart of it, the heart of the whole thing, banishing poetry and banishing the poet, the greatest of them all because he is the greatest, banishing Homer for telling lies, for telling bad lies because of the power of Homer's art to charm, to seduce you with the honeyed muse of epic verse and lyric verse, to nourish emotions and passions in men instead of restraint, of law and reason what we've been arguing from the start isn't it? These lies and fictions of the, getting a little confused get my legs straight steady myself against the, careful? Good God, this heap goes I'd go with it never get up again just, slowly yes that's the danger, this honeyed muse painting inferior views of truth even her sister arts of imitation stacking the deck he'll let her back in, let our sweet friend back in if she'll prove her right to exist in his orderly state, be pleasant and useful to humanity it's all, getting things backward I'm, get my arm behind the careful! Backed myself into a corner here stripping the naked animal clean among, among images of moral deformity? What was that about musical training about the piano, the phantom hands not what I remember no, use my memory to get myself oriented here but I can't remember, can't remember can't even remember what I was trying to remember back to training your memory, back to Pythagoras' school of recollection train your memory to remember the sins and suffering of the, of the muses the daughters of memory of accurate memory of an actual vision from somewhere deep in the oh, oh, oh no yes don't move no, carefully whole thing's, whole thing's slipping don't, very, very slowly don't, no. No! no no no help! Oh my, my God oh my God! Just, hold on just hold on to something or I'll go with it just, no! Help! The whole heap it's, good God all over the floor try to, try not to move get my breath sweating and shaking my face is wet it's wet I'm, look at it. All over the floor the whole, look! Look there's Dodds knew I'd brought it, knew I had it if I can let my, if I can stand up and no! Good God no, whole trash heap all over the floor go down and I'd be part of the trash heap. I can't, wait where's my pencil! I can't, sweat stinging my eyes whole thing's a blur out there hardly see across the room maybe I, spilled some papers on the bed here got to find it, got to find my pencil don't write it down I'll lose it maybe already lost it might be under the, find that towel yes clean myself up before I no, good God look at it! How could, all going backward braced myself against that heap like a pillar of salt whole thing yes, the unswerving punctuality of chance, clock without the clockmaker perfectly simple in word and deed says Plato, God wouldn't lie or change because he's perfect so it's God God God, virtue and beauty and no mad or senseless person can be God's friend no, make yourselves eunuchs for the kingdom of heaven's sake says Tolstoy, nothing senseless about that is there? Strive for absolute chastity for the good of the neighborhood whole purpose of life to be part of God's kingdom only way to get there's absolute chastity, husband and wife live like brother and sister nothing mad about that is there? Dress up like a muzhik float around the house look like Noah's Ark whole performance out of the greatest fiction ever created, take God out of the equation you've got nothing left not even love no, had that somewhere if I had that letter Wagner wrote to Röckel where love's lost sight of because everything we do, think, take and give is in fear of the end, the greatest most desperate fiction of the afterlife ever created yes, the denial of death, what this whole mad escapade's all about, isn't it Levochka? Good God how you fight it! Your man Pozdnyshev in The Kreutzer Sonata wallowing in the slime of debauchery he tells us, keeps stripping away the fictions right down to what it's really all about and then he can't face it, not just love no, only you, the choice of one man or woman over all others says the lady on the train won't have it will you, Pozdnyshev. Supposed to be something noble and ideal but it's just something sordid that brings us down to the level of pigs. Natural? a natural human activity? No no no, eating's natural, something you enjoy but this is unnatural and loathsome, honeymoon's shameful and tedious, nothing sacred for us about marriage nothing to it but copulation, couple of months you've learned to hate the sight of each other ready to poison her or shoot yourself good God man, when you felt the blade go into her didn't what it's really all about stare you in the face? Some nonsense there about mankind following some ideal that's the fiction isn't it? What Plato's poets and honeyed muse are all about, you strip it clean stop short and run because you really know don't you, not like pigs and rabbits reproducing themselves as fast as they can but you hold it at arm's length, even say animals seem to know their offspring mean survival of the species while you wonder if life has a purpose and that's it isn't it! That you're being used, used, used, that you're being used by nature simply to perpetuate the family line, the social tribe, the white race, the species just like your pigs and rabbits and that's what you resent, what you hate, what you go through hell for and she knew it too didn't she? Knew what her body was for, like animals know yes and she knew you thought you owned her body, why you're terrified by a woman bearing down on you in a ballgown because you know those bare arms and shoulders, you know those breasts aren't just playthings she's offering to you posing as an instrument of pleasure but bigger the better there's gallons, there's the promise of gallons of survival of the species like a yes, like a huge brood mare. Pleasure yes, yes it's beautifully done jealousy and the whole un, unreasonable the whole madness when the what was his name, the violinist Trukhachev God knows what shows up nice looking with a yes, yes I remember this with a well developed posterior? Like a woman yes like Hottentots they tell you with a talent they tell you for music and we're off for music yes, for music the cause of it all? Him and your wife bound together by music, "the most refined form of sensual lust" you call it? The cause of most of the adulteries in your class of society? A fearful thing but what is it? That description you put in somewhere Pozdnyshev, it's lovely, that music carries you off into another state of being that's not your own, of feeling things you don't really feel, of understanding things you don't really understand, of being able to do things you aren't really able to do it's everything we've been talking about from the start, discover your unsuspected talent, you can play better by roll than many who play by hand, the biggest thrill in music is playing it yourself even untrained persons can do it, it's your participation that rouses your emotions most, these phantom hands, this detachable self, Homer's dangerous demon with its own life and energy you can't control force you to do things you wouldn't otherwise, everything Plato wants to banish, scrape away every fiction get down to the truth, to the naked animal banish them yes, banish the Lydian mode and the Ionian and the flute above all the flute worse than all the strings together invented for nothing but pleasure and Homer, banish Homer and all of the poets and painters and sculptors whose love poems and naked Venuses celebrate women as instruments of pleasure take that first movement of The Kreutzer Sonata, the presto you say, can we allow it to be played in a drawing room full of women in lowcut dresses? Good God Pozdnyshev and we're back where we started, where pleasure in all circumstances is bad, we're here to be punished and we ought to be punished so you've killed your wife and her Hottentot suitor with musical tastes escapes under the piano, is all this simply an outburst of the passions and emotions Plato wants to save us from censoring practically banishing the arts or is it, is it a stew of disease and impairment, madness and suicide that produces the artist, Keats consumptive and Beethoven deaf, Dostoevsky epileptic, Byron's foot and Homer's blindness if he existed at all,

Baudelaire and Schiller and enough madness and suicide to please God himself, Schumann and Kleist suicides, Hölderlin insane and the most agonizing of them all of course yes, sitting there empty eyed in a white gown on exhibit for his loathsome sister's teatime guests, wasn't that she'd betrayed the man, the artist, sold him out no that's to be expected, he's expendable, just the vehicle or the husk of it for the work that's what she betrayed, that's our immortality and that's what she corrupted, worse than murder Pozdnyshev, worse than murder you can ask your master Pozdnyshev and take comfort, yes, of all people, Tolstoy of all artists of all suicides manqués Levochka would agree. She's just been widowed by a blazing anti-Semite suicide herself and here's dear brother fresh out of the madhouse and long out of the spell of his most famous friend he believed to be Germany's greatest creative genius, good God Pozdnyshev! If you were playing the "Pilgrims' Chorus," how much would it mean to you to have the composer Richard Wagner himself by your side? Great Wagner comes and, lifting them aloft above the clouds, transports them to the mighty halls of old Walhalla in Ride of Walkyries taking this poisonous anti-Semitic little woman with him. No more wooden fingers no but phantom hands, she seizes the rights to all her stupefied brother's work published and unpublished, unfinished ideas, notes and letters, even letters to his mother she alters and forges addressed to herself and comes out with a completely corrupted pasted together jumble called The Will to Power as his final work, the blond beast and ruthlessly distorted superman orchestrating the blackest period in German history, you see? His immortality that's what she corrupted, his glorious vision in his early book The Birth of Tragedy where Apollo's classic Greek power to create measured and harmonious beauty is endlessly assailed by the drunken frenzy of Dionysus threatening to smash everything the sheer, the sheer tension the energy the tinge of madness, the supernatural powers that emerge, from disease that Plato mentions and the primitive idea that crazy people speak in divine languages and above all yes above all the catharsis of abandoned music and dance we've talked about that haven't we, should have looked into that yourself Pozdnyshev, should have tried it. Should have learned the tango Pozdnyshev, the most elegant, merciless, disciplined abandon never would have killed her, learned the tango you never would have killed her and if I had I wouldn't be here now, listen. Listen where's my clothes, can you help me? Ought to go out and get some fresh air, get out of this dim suffocating airless lightless little no no wait not yet no, these demons of Homer's and Golyadkin's doppelgänger who's gone with his bed in the morning when Petrushka brings in tea and explains that his master's not at home shouting You idiot Petrushka! I'm your master!! Can't get away, each one of them haunting the Other, hounding the Other, following him everywhere with his piercing terrifying glare and a few vicious remarks enough to drive a man mad, moves in with him moves out to some dirty little hotel room like this one but follows him home like a dog finally simply has to end it, simply has to get rid of the Other, he wasn't mine was he? He was my fiction wasn't he? Not easy no but it's got to be done, my creation wasn't it? Like Levochka thinking your thoughts so you can have them? Lie back here and see things falling into place like reading the Tarot, no reason that betrayal can't be positive is there? Beautiful little innocent climbs into my lap fell on my neck with kisses while we put together this fiction of appearing as the nonperson my joy! My honeyed muse, my sometime daughter, scraping it away now for the real nonperson here because there's finally no getting around it is there. Because what I've been dreading, what I've feared, what got me here in the first place no surgery no but this, this hormonal chemical God knows what treatment has put me out of business, out of being a threat yes maybe I never was. Maybe I never was! That was the great betrayal wasn't it, where it all started, and everywhere the ceremony of innocence was drowned. Listen. Can you, can you pull a shade over there? The sun's getting in my eyes, sitting still here in a room God knows these shadows of the real state we're all living in, dim shapes, those weightless shadows the chorus held up to Ajax in his slaughterhouse survive now simply as gossip like everything else in the end where they'll say I never really planned the whole property transfer to them out of love but just as a scheme to avoid taxes? Where they'll say I'm the one who betrayed my daughters because I'd really surrendered nothing, the baby king who tyrannizes through the sheer blackmail of his existence, that I betrayed them and you and everyone yes, the artist as confidence man that I betrayed even myself from the fear of trying to carry the unforgiving burden of the real artist, to try to hide the failure of everything I'd promised there left stranded, like some maiden aunt's Torschlusspanik at being left unmarried on the shelf, art and entertainment and technology, of authenticity and the true story of its philosopher corrupted by his sister as gossip of the most sinister sort, of love as the ultimate fiction and music the most refined form of Levochka's sensual lust building up like the pressure of steam that would burst the boiler if the safety valve of sex didn't release it he tells us in that frenzied metaphor of mechanization reaching everywhere, of art without the artist as a threat and the end of him at the twist of a knife but it wasn't that crude, no. No it doesn't really matter because that's what gossip does, isn't that what gossip is? Dawn breaking on the handsome face of mortal youth, verweile doch! du bist so schön the goddess asking immortality for him like her immortal own but the legs have crumbled, pursued by age as punishment for pleasure and all of it fading into that bed of shades, those imitations and shadowy images of gossip where there is no present moment but only the next one being devoured in the immense maw of the past, where immortality finds its home at last, where the voice has dwindled to the dry scratch of a grasshopper and the legs are gone, they're just not there and it all comes down in a heap good God look at them! Blood dried on the sheets and those damn rusting staples don't know whether I'm shivering or shaking from the, try to find one dry corner down there. Try to sit up and get one leg down where it's, something down there, just get my arm so I can reach the, whole sodden mess look at that. Mel-O-Dee Music Rolls, Mel-O-Art, QRS Campaign Against Filth in Popular Songs they sold a million rolls in 1926. Sell more Player Rolls! Sell more Player Pianos! Sell More Ukuleles and Banjos! More! More! More! God it was so it was all so America! It was the crowd, not the dry scratch of the grasshopper but the herd, it was "the little people making merry like grasshoppers in spots of sunlight, hardly thinking" just perpetuating the species weren't they? "Foolishly reduplicating folly in thirty-year periods; they eat and they laugh too." Groan against elitism, against Flaubert in retreat, "I believe that the crowd, the mass, the herd, will always be detestable" he writes to George Sand, remember? When he's written his niece preparing his Paris flat before his death, "I ask to be liberated from my enemy, the piano, and from another enemy, which hits me on the forehead—the stupid hanging lamp in the dining room" and weeks later, de Maupassant to Turgenev,

"Flaubert apoplexy, no hope" where nothing survives of importance "save a small group of minds, ever the same, which pass on the torch." No more piano! I said. Absolutely no artist! By now electricity is spreading its blessings everywhere, from refinements on the reproducing piano with the, where, in Germany? No that was my invention wasn't it? Wrote it down yes and somebody stole it? The reproducing piano is made possible by an electric motor attached to the pump providing constant and predetermined air pressure, while back at home here the electric player with a magnet for each key appears, the nickel in the slot making the electrical contact pounding out its mechanical note; missing some in bad weather, but still in the vanguard other public entertainment a murderer named Kemmler provides material for the first electrocution at Auburn Prison. Progress! Great God wherever you'd look says Reverend Newell Dwight Hillis, "For the first time government, invention, art, industry, and religion have served all the people rather than the patrician classes." Wait a minute no, no not so fast Reverend, elitists staging a rearguard action here, Steinway brings Paderewski over here and Knabe opens Carnegie Hall with Tchaikovsky live, piano makers and European patrons supporting music and the arts as diversions for Plato's patricians and disdaining American artists as rubes who disdain them as foreign laborers. Whole thing coming to pieces here, just to get it over with but, with what? Over with what? Prepositions make all the trouble but you can't really explain anything to anybody why I've got to explain all this because we don't know how much time's left to finish this work of mine before it's distorted and turned into a cartoon because it is a cartoon for that herd out there, the crowd, the mass waiting to be entertained, turn the creative artist into a performer because they are the hallucination, you see? The whole thing's turned upside down, the kittens are bit and the houses are built without walls, you see? Used to be the reality was the stone Doctor Johnson kicked and Doctor Johnson himself, and hallucinations took place in the head, in the mind, now everything out there is the hallucination and the mind where the work is done is the only reality, because the work is the only refuge from this torn wet-smelling hallucination of the body looks like a, like some map all fingered and latticed see right through it where the Great Lakes with that biggest one hanging down like some immense weak malformed invertebrate fit only to be whipped, so if reality is the work when it goes wrong all that's waiting out there is the sweat, the blood and, problem where's the blood coming from, not bleeding anywhere but I keep finding fresh blood on the, not even on the collar no under the collar like a vampire? Nothing mystical about all this it's not some half-baked Buddhist nirvana where all is illusion good God no, because the rage is there at the heart of it, the sheer energy, the sheer tension the tinge of madness where the work gets done, the only reality, the only refuge from the vast hallucination that's everything out there, and that you're all part of out there where everything equals everything else. Ten, a hundred, a thousand years ago it's all one, where immortality becomes gossip, 1890 van Gogh shoots himself in a wheat field, Rimbaud's gone the next year, and so is Melville and to even things out Whitman a year later Rudolf Diesel invents the internal combustion engine, Eastman Kodak is founded in his mother's kitchen tainted by gossip over just where he got the idea for flexible film and Thomas Edison celebrates entertainment and art and the ascendancy of the crowd, the herd, with the patent on the kinetoscope, you see? Carnegie the working man's friend locks him out and goes fishing in Scotland to avoid the death and carnage at Homestead so it's Frick who gets stabbed, pushpin or Pushkin long since killed in a duel and it's all one, everything out there it's all this grand hallucination where Count Tolstoy is stalking Turgenev, following him everywhere with his piercing frightening glare enough to drive a man mad with vicious remarks Turgenev tells a friend and he's weeping again, remember? Being haunted by this Other we've been talking about, The Kreutzer Sonata's been banned here why? because Beethoven's German? But it's not the World War when Wagner's music was banned here no, no this goes back to the day Wagner's art was damned as "nothing more than the dope required by a decadent generation" by his disciple, his apostle, by the one who believed him to be Germany's greatest creative genius, by the, good God can't you see? Wagner was the Other, he was the where is that, Michelangelo and the Self who could do more because that's what it's all about so he had to be killed, Nietzsche had to kill him and be carried away to an asylum a year later, while great Wagner lifts us aloft above the clouds to the mighty halls of old Walhalla where these great artists will never play again, but their phantom hands will live forever,

haunt us forever. Forever! Good God that's, question's whether all this clatter and bang, old Walhalla
and Chin Chin Temple Bells preserved on piano rolls
are part of the hallucination or only escape from it,
see what was going on everywhere out there in this
frenzy of invention more than a century ago? In Germany the Ariston player with thirty-six notes then
the Hupfeld with sixty-one still no pneumatics till
the Welte family patents its pneumatic Orchestrion
operated with a perforated paper roll, in France Car-
pentier shows his Melograph and Melotrope to the
French Academy, mechanical fingers brought to life
by electromagnets and a perforated strip. But before
that France had claimed credit for the whole thing
with Fourneaux's pneumatic Pianista, its fingers
worked through a piece of pierced cardboard, and
here? Peel off these damn notes sticking together
worse than I am just the smell and all the rest of it,
half the time inventing half the time litigating,
Kelly invents a wind motor with slide valves opening and closing ports with electrical help, Merritt
Gally's inventions fighting on both fronts, R W Pain
and Henry Kuster build Needham & Sons their first
pneumatic piano player that's half as big as the piano
it attacks, somebody else is making a folding piano

that's portable and there's the Piano écran that can be used as a screen or set up as a card table I mean all that's got to be part of the hallucination doesn't it? Look. There's more to it, all that beating the bushes out there there's more to it there's a, a hunger that hasn't taken shape haunting the whole thing. It's not just mother tapping the parlour piano note by note with her illustrated song The Little Lost Child or one of a hundred more about lost children, orphaned children, sick children, all in plentiful supply no, there's more to it. More what! Are you crazy? You think some phantom hand some, some significant Other will burst out of the bushes and redeem any shred of value hidden in your grand hallucination? Provide some refuge from it where your reality prevails? Where the work gets done? Yes and why not! Because right now it finds its despairing voice in a novel that sweeps the nation, when Peter Ibbetson would "buy or beg or borrow the music that had filled me with such emotion and delight, and take it home to my little square piano, and try to finger it out for myself. But I had begun too late in life. To sit, longing and helpless, before an instrument one cannot play, with a lovely score one cannot read!" Yes and then at that moment what, deliverance? A patent issued for the Angelus Piano Player that can be played by hand or automatically with its mechanism working at the rear end of the keys not interfering with anything. You see? Why that novel of du Maurier's was a rage in America where the biggest thrill in music would be in playing it yourself, what we talked about back at the start of all this? Where it's your own participation that rouses your emotions most? Where you can play better by roll than many who play by hand, where you can play all pieces while they can play but a few? And isn't that your significant Other who cut the roll in the first place? Your self who can do more yes, these phantom hands that transform you into this Other, not talking about those detachable selves that can be withdrawn from the body we talked about, no. Not like the bellytalkers or doppelgängers, Golyadkin pursuing his doppelgänger or Golyadkin's doppelgänger pursuing Golyadkin no, more like one of those dangerous demons of Homer's with lives and energies of their own that aren't really part of you since you can't control them. And now even untrained persons can do it! Back with Plato's chance persons pouring out Für Elise without a flaw till the last perforation in the roll passes over the corresponding hole in the tracker bar and democracy comes lumbering into the room with the piano player hunched over the keyboard half as big as the piano itself. It's all like, it's like a kind of plagiary, like Gottschalk composing his bar room player piano music fifty years before the player was invented, like my own ideas being stolen before I even had them since I'm clearly the one person qualified for a piece of work like this one, first because I can't read music and can't play anything but a comb. Second because I use only secondhand material which any court would dismiss as hearsay so we can reduce it to gossip like everything else, and finally. Finally I really don't believe any of it. You see? I don't really believe you can take ninety-six people, that's almost two hundred hands, take out some of them like the sleigh bells there's still more than a hundred-odd hands doing entirely different things, guiding bows across strings pressing the neck so fast it's dizzying, fingers pushing, plunging valves, keys opening holes and closing them, the clarinet changing whole registers translating every jot and tittle on the score into a stab, a wail, a delicate lonely suspense, a blast to wake the dead, sforzando, piano God knows what all of it going on at once but not exactly all at once because what's coming out of all this is a

Pastoral Symphony, what's rising to the heavens is Bruckner's Eighth or Mozart's D Minor Piano Concerto, what overwhelms the senses is Eliot's "music heard so deeply That it is not heard at all, but you are the music While the music lasts" but isn't that then, isn't that the hallucination? Transforming this chaos of hands guiding bows, fingers plunging valves resolving this clutter of physical of, you see? I can't think about it, I can't not think about it but when I try not to think about it I go absolutely crazy but that's, no. Can you hear me? Listen. Start back with these three wait, two pianos, first the enemy Flaubert asked to be liberated from. No more piano! I said, only that small group of minds, ever the same, to pass on the torch. And the second one, Peter Ibbetson's enigmatic little square piano that will not surrender its secrets, leaving him helpless before an instrument he cannot play, a score he can't read, finding its author one day walking across Hampstead Heath with Henry James and a new idea for a story, begging the American novelist to write it, good God what it might have turned into in James's delicate hands! But James handed it back yes and here's the third one, the third piano, a big semigrand by Broadwood, brought to Paris by La Petite Vitesse freshly tuned for the hands of the man once the best pianist of his time at the Leipzig Conservatory, but now fallen to poverty and deceit, borrowing money, betraying and cheating anyone in reach, bullying anyone less talented, that is to say everyone, in the name of the art which he still holds bitterly sacred, supplying his miserable needs with any dodge he can devise, treating a young woman suffering from severe pain with an approach floating up from central Europe, where my golden Sigi had opened the era of psychoanalysis with a paper on the psychological mechanism of hysteria and was already embracing "free association" to replace hypnosis, left in the hands of those who've departed most lamentably from his own ideal most ably represented by the scapegrace now seated on the divan opposite the suffering girl looking at him fixed in the whites of his eyes. He passed a hand on her forehead and temples, and down her cheek and her throat till her eyes closed and her face emptied. Was she still in pain? Oh! presque plus du tout, monsieur! she cries out and he, stunned by the shock of her cri du coeur ringing in the rafters, asks to look into her mouth, finding its roof like the dome of the Panthéon with room for toutes les gloires de la France, its entrance like the middle porch of Saint Sulpice, not a tooth missing, the bridge of her nose like the belly of a Stradivarius, what a sounding board! She must come back to be cured of her pain when it returns, he will play Schubert and her voice will be trained, meanwhile she shall see nothing, hear nothing, think of nothing, think of nothing but Svengali, Svengali, Svengali! And the world at large but America in extravagant particular would hear nothing, talk of nothing, read nothing, but Trilby, Trilby, Trilby, nothing but the inevitable stage production of Trilby where even the soft felt hat worn there became and is still called a trilby. People went trilby mad. You had to be there. Can you hear me? The America of discovering your hidden talent, of self-improvement, of one born every minute. Over there, dying Offenbach's one wish, to see the premiere of his Tales of Hoffmann, had come a year too late with its mechanical dolls by Spalanzani passing off one as his daughter for poor Hoffmann to fall in love with, and a girl in act three who sings herself to death. But three years? Svengali and a friend teaching Trilby eight hours a day morning noon and night for three years, violin and Svengali with his little flageolet, Gott im Himmel! Wieder zurück! The most astoundingly beautiful sounds ever heard from a human throat, one note drawn through all the colors of the rainbow as Svengali's eyes directed her, the greatest contralto, the greatest soprano the world had ever known till that terrible night in Drury Lane when Svengali died in the box opposite and it was all over. Can you hear me? I'm, no, get my breath can't get my breath, what it's all about anyhow, that note drawn through the rainbow as his eyes directed this Other he had created feel like myself just the breathing, the breathing the, not being able to, to make these wonderful sounds he'd wanted and nothing else, to think his thoughts and wish his wishes, all of it nothing but Svengali's love for himself turned inside out wasn't it, yes! Yes and that, where did that come from! Finally yes that, where it's all been going from the start, that cry from Michelangelo, O Dio, o Dio, o Dio, Chi m'a tolto a me stesso Ch'a me fusse più presso O più di me potessi, che poss' io? O Dio, o Dio, who has taken the one closest to me who could do more than no, no it's not that pedestrian it's fifteenth, sixteenth century Italian nearer poetry, Who nearer to me Or more mighty yes, more mighty than I Tore me away from myself. Tore me away! che poss', what can I do? I'll tell you che poss' io! Get him back, whoever took this Other, tore away the closest to me who could do more yes wheel up the player, put a roll in and start pumping all trying to get out from under this cumbersome damn thing with its tiny fingers get a fine burnished player inside a case, a cocoon, says one pupa to the other as a butterfly passes, you'd never get me into an outfit like that, O Dio, o Dio, odious, repugnant, from odium, hatred, odisse to hate God the bedmaker you hear me Svengali? That old friendship between myself and myself broken by age coming on, left my ideas and opinions to suit public opinion and be part of it a, a yes a nonperson looking back at the arrogant self-made self when you were the finest pianist at the Leipzig Conservatory before it was torn from you, before your love of singing became a croak in your throat and before you became Trilby's Self who could do more till Age finally took you and the magnificent voice that we'd heard, that the world had heard when she sang the Impromptu was yours wasn't it Svengali! You singing with her voice, wasn't it! Age withering arrogant youth and worse, the works of arrogant youth and the book I wrote then, my first book, it's become my enemy, o Dio, odium, the rage and energy and boundless excitement the only reality where the work that's become my enemy got done and the only refuge from the hallucination that's everything out there is the greater one that transforms you good God, Pozdnyshev, those words that Levochka gave you to transform the whole thing when "music carries you off into another state of being that's not your own, of feeling things you don't really feel, of understanding things you don't really understand, of being able to do things you aren't really able to do" yes, that transforms that transfigures you yourself into the self who can do more! That was Youth with its reckless exuberance when all things were possible pursued by Age where we are now, looking back at what we destroyed, what we tore away from that self who could do more, and its work that's become my enemy because that's what I can tell you about, that Youth who could do anything.

AFTERWORD

Joseph Tabbi

Agapē Agape is William Gaddis's swan song, his most concentrated fiction, and the one work where he risks a direct address to the reader. The distillation of a project that occupied him throughout his professional life, this final fiction began as an exhaustive social history of the player piano in America, whose lineaments can be read in the thousands of notes, clippings, working papers, drafts, and snippets that Gaddis left at his death. Organized roughly, like all of his manuscripts and background materials, into numbered cardboard boxes, the remains of his research match the narrative description: among the working papers, one finds a chronology from the player's invention in 1876 to 1929, "when the player piano world and everything else collapsed." Handwritten reminders, in a hand whose changes can be discerned over half a century, appear in the margins, or on whatever scraps of paper he had around. "Chaos theory as a means toward order," reads one note among the strips and folders that Gaddis would refer to when composing his last work. After a career spent imagining in detail the vast systems and multiple voices of an emerging global culture—in works that have themselves been called "systems novels"[1]—Gaddis at the end would reflect primarily on his own private system of assembling materials and putting words down on paper.

As with all of his books, for *Agapē Agape* much of the working material was cut out from popular magazines and newspapers. (Even the high literature, art, music, and technology references that made him seem forbiddingly "erudite" to some readers often came out of daily papers, or this material was sent to him by acquaintances; possibly more came to him this way than from books.) Often, Gaddis would combine strips on a single topic or under a single date and tape them all the way along one side, on a single long page. When correcting galleys and typescripts, he would insert words and small phrases by hand, but he preferred to lay in new material in typed strips cut with scissors. Composition, for Gaddis, was a distinctly material practice, involving a literal organization and arrangement of found materials, even as his narrator struggles literally to hold himself together. In a sense, the writer becomes the page on which he's writing: the wreck of an old man in *Agapē* has rusting staples in his legs, and his skin is like tissue paper from the drugs he's been taking. He worries that his books will be left on the shelf, unread, while his unpublished research molders in the boxes stacked around him. But as long as he goes on reading, revising, adding to the manuscript, he will stave off death and madness and keep the work from becoming "what it's about": entropy, chaos, loss, and a mechanized culture indifferent to the cultivation of particular, individual talents.

This is the theme he would come back to, obsessively, in the very last working papers and at the last page of *Agapē:* "Discover yr hidden talent," "yr unsuspected talent," "disc secret talent" all appear on one page of notes, along with "the self who could do more" (three times, with variations). The notetaking evidently continued weeks and months past the time when he'd declared the manuscript finished—confirming a lifelong habit he had of writing past a book's end. That's how it went with *The Recognitions,* which Gaddis completed half a century before, when he still had on his desk pages of "outlined notes . . . for spinning out the novel's conclusion" (letter to Steven Moore, April 7, 1983). And the succeeding books each took off, in their turn, from the leftover drafts of work that preceded it until, at the end of his life, Gaddis determined to transform his accumulated research into one gemlike meditation without false illusions or consolations.

The player-piano history, had it been completed, would have been an impressive coda to the fiction. As scholarship, it would have put Gaddis belatedly in the tradition of those North American writers on media and technology—Lewis Mumford, Elizabeth Eisenstein, Marshall McLuhan, and Neil Postman—who could perceive technology's aesthetic consequences and wellsprings. As literary criticism, much of what Gaddis intended had already been accomplished by Hugh Kenner in *The Counterfeiters.* As a conceptual work, the history could scarcely have rivaled Walter Benjamin's "Work of Art in the Age of Mechanical Reproduction." Gaddis knew this; he knew that his contribution to the study of mechanization and the arts had already been accomplished, indirectly, with his novels. But the accumulated research of half a century weighed on him during these final years, demanding an outlet. He worked hard on the history through 1996 and early 1997, when he discovered that he would not have long to live. By that time, however, he had already decided to reformat the work as a fiction, having finally realized that his own raillery on the subject was more interesting to him than "a dim pursuit of scholarship headed for the same trash heap I'm upset about in the first place."[2]

Once he had finally set aside the history, Gaddis used his boxes of snippets to create a character who had an obsession identical with his own, whose lived experience and efforts at composition could dramatize both the possibilities and "the destructive element" within an emerging technological order. Later, in 1998, when he was commissioned by DeutschlandRadio to write a play suitable for broadcasting, he responded with a fragment unlike anything he—or anyone else—had ever written: a one-act monologue entitled *Torschlusspanik* (the fear of doors closing, of opportunities lost, of staying single, and—not least—of going unread). The work was translated and broadcast on March 3, 1999, three and a half months after Gaddis died. At his death, a somewhat longer typescript of eighty-four pages, intended by Gaddis for posthumous publication, was sent to his agent under the same title he had used for the history: *Agapē Agape.* His last words sound and read less like a deathbed utterance than a posthumous one, from beyond the grave—less a lament, finally, for his own passing than an honest expression of fear at where technology is taking the world.

A Secret History of *Agapē Agape*

The voice Gaddis found for his last fiction is unique but not without literary precedent. In the early nineties, Gaddis had discovered the works of Thomas Bernhard, and he sensed in this near contemporary from Austria not only personal affinities but a model for his reconceived project, a minimalism that allowed him to transform (rather than abandon) his accumulated research. The shift from scholarship to fiction would be accomplished by giving musical form to the work itself. Rather than reiterate music history, Gaddis would invite the reader to experience the work's musicality; his lifework would be understood not by following his labor and his logic, but through listening to his voice and its several modulations. Bernhard's musicologist in his novel *Concrete,* writing a biography of Mendelssohn-Bartholdy, aims at a "major work of impeccable scholarship" that would leave "far behind it and far beneath it everything else, both published and unpublished," that he had ever written.[3] Gaddis at a high moment may have felt the same about his player-piano history; most of the time he more likely suspected that his research would ultimately be left to "some beleaguered doctoral candidate"—as he said to me in a letter of 1989.

The Loser and *Concrete* are not only cited by Gaddis; they provide narrative models, or, as Gaddis's narrator would say, plagiarisms in advance, "like my own ideas being stolen before I even had them." Bernhard's subjects were Gaddis's subjects also—musicology, home-state excoriation, and Glenn Gould as the hidden talent who could do more than his fellow students, Wertheimer and Bernard's narrator in *The Loser,* causing both of them to give up piano playing. Also, the brevity of Bernhard's work was made to order for Gaddis's reformatted fiction—this and the single narrative voice capacious enough to express subtle shifts in mood and occasional surges. More specifically still, this stripped-down style was consistent with the effects of prednisone—the drug that both Gaddis and Bernhard had taken for relief from emphysema. To his son Matthew, Gaddis would recall waking up singing after his first use of the drug, and its jag is consistent with the peculiar pacing of the narrative he left us—its meandering, hallucinatory quality that suddenly comes to a focus on one particular object, one item within the field of vision capable of absorbing attention and momentarily freeing the body from pain and breathlessness.

Bernhard is certainly a far cry from the meganovelists—Pynchon, Joyce, Melville—whom critics usually associate with Gaddis. But the fiction Gaddis cites with affection and admiration—du Maurier's *Trilby,* Tolstoy's *Kreutzer Sonata,* John Kennedy Toole's *Confederacy of Dunces*—and his public expressions of admiration for the talkative novels of Saul Bellow and Norman O. Douglas should widen the literary context within which his own body of work might now be read and appreciated. What he particularly admired in Bernhard—and in writers as diverse as Joan Didion and Evelyn Waugh—was the economy of style, the ability to write ex-

pansively without wasting words. That stripped-down quality was just as important to Gaddis's own aesthetic as the
highbrow satire (in Douglas and Waugh), the entropic vision
(in Didion's *Slouching Toward Bethlehem*), or the apocalyptic
destruction in Yeats's "Second Coming" (a favorite poem of
Gaddis's, whose high-toned mysticism he had once dismissed
but then came to appreciate after reading Didion[4]). Unique
as *Agapē* may be, it should attune readers to qualities of voice
and economies of style that have largely gone unnoticed in
Gaddis's earlier work.

Where the continuities between the earlier and later fiction stand out most clearly is in Gaddis's previous depictions
of artists and writers—characters who, through their appetite
for destruction and self-destruction, fail on their own terms.
"Overwhelmed by the material demands" their art imposes,
these characters—as Gaddis said in an interview in 1987—
generally fail "to pursue the difficult task for which their talents have equipped them."[5] Most often they cannot focus
their energies and—like Gaddis at work on the player-piano
project—they have trouble finishing things. In his second
novel, *J R*, Gaddis would show Jack Gibbs working fruit-
lessly on sections from Gaddis's own early drafts for the project. Another character in *J R*, Thomas Eigen, like Gaddis has
written an unpublished play on the Civil War, and this same
play, entitled "Once at Antietem," would be recast and
worked into the structure of Gaddis's fourth novel, *A Frolic of
His Own*. Recycling his own work, and the work of others,
was consistent with Gaddis's overall aesthetic—he was, in
many senses, an ecological novelist who at the end cringes to

think of "what we destroyed" and who could not bear to see things wasted—not money, not talent, and certainly not the unpublished products of his own creative energies.

At the end of his life, by concentrating his epic research into a novella, Gaddis was following a pattern he had already worked out for still another persona in *J R,* the young composer Edward Bast. Unable to ward off the demands and distractions of life in corporate America—the materialistic world of "brokers, bankers, salesmen, factory workers, most politicians, the lot"—Bast undergoes a gradual reduction of his musical ambitions. As Gaddis said in the 1987 interview:

> Bast starts with great confidence . . . , that confidence of youth. He's going to write grand opera. And gradually, if you noticed . . . , his ambitions shrink. The grand opera becomes a cantata where we have the orchestra and the voices. Then it becomes a piece for orchestra, then a piece for small orchestra, and finally at the end he's writing a piece for unaccompanied cello, his own that is to say, one small voice trying to rescue it all and say, "Yes, there *is* hope."[6]

In Bast, too, Gaddis concentrated "that romantic intoxication" at once ridiculous and wonderful which had seen him through the composition of *The Recognitions*—a book whose successful completion (and initial commercial failure) haunts the historical project that Gaddis returned to, fifty years later, in *Agapē Agape.*

Instead of a self-generated cosmos to place over against the material universe, Gaddis imagines this "one small voice"—

although it is easily lost in so vast and noisy a novel as *J R.* Now that the voice has been isolated and made to speak out in *Agapē Agape,* readers might arrive at a fuller appreciation of what Gaddis was trying to do in his lifelong literary engagement with the materials, systems, and specialized languages of corporate America. The single voice that emerges out of competing voices and constraining media is not only the voice of "artistic individualism" struggling vainly against commodification by the capitalist machine.[7] Gaddis does not fool himself into imagining that he can oppose his art's power to the power of the material world. What he can do, however, is to coordinate his art with the vast systems and structures that now shape our world. And we, in turn, can fashion new images of ourselves within that world by reading, by listening, and by attending to how these multiple voices and worldly materials have been heard and organized by the author.

Rather than opposing an artistic individualism against an impersonal, collectivist technology, Gaddis investigates their common historical roots as creative collaborations. From Vaucanson's mechanical loom for figured silks to Jacquard to the drum roll on the player piano to the punched data card in the first computers: in part, the digital age owes its existence to the arts. Yet Gaddis, who continued to tear out and save anything he came across on the subject, found scant acknowledgment of technology's debt. The "frenzy of invention" that culminated in the player piano in 1876 seemed intent, rather, on removing the artist from the arts altogether, just as the century ahead sought to eliminate the very possibility of human failure as a condition for success in the arts. "Analysis, measurement, prediction and control, the elimination of failure through programmed organization"—Gaddis had set the terms and cultural context for a "secret history of the player piano" as early as the 1960s, when the double-take-inducing title, *Agapē Agape,* first appears in his papers. The title turns up again in *J R,* as the unfinished "social history of mechanization and the arts" that overwhelms Jack Gibbs by becoming what it's about: "the destructive element." *Agapē*— the community of brotherly love celebrated by early Christian writers—has come apart (agape) through mechanization and a technological democracy that reduces art to the level of light entertainment, a spectacle for the gaze of the masses. Ultimately, the "vast hallucination that's everything out there and that you're all part of"—Gaddis addresses his readers here directly—derives from nothing but little gaps, sprockets in a film strip, patterns of holes in paper.

Through all his research on the player piano, Gaddis relentlessly documents an American culture of simulation in which technology has become the only imaginable solution to problems it created in the first place. The same demonic circularity that can sometimes put computer operators "at the mercy of the systems they've designed" would inform his narrative of a mind devouring itself in endless self-reflection. But something happens near the end of *Agapē* that enables Gaddis to imagine an escape from the technological hall of mirrors. Hurried by the sense of his impending death, and finally unable to avoid identification with the biological, abject, material "Other" of his imagination, Gaddis risks a direct personal address—to the reader, and to the ghosts, demons, philosophers, and fictional characters he holds in conversation. This identification with his "detachable selves" makes possible the astonishing final pages, when the man in the bed speaks, evidently without irony or satirical intent, of what he has been able to hold in belief: "Finally I really don't believe any of it," except for the evidence of the senses and memory and now, when they are to be lost, in the reality of the youthful "self who could do more," and its work.

"The self who could do more": this phrase from a verse by Michelangelo appears in every one of Gaddis's books: *"O Dio, o Dio, o Dio, / Chi m'a tolto a me stesso / Ch'a me fusse più presso / O più di me potessi, che poss' io?"* Rejecting the standard translation[8] as pedestrian, Gaddis near the end of *Agapē* offers a version of his own: "It's fifteenth, sixteenth century Italian nearer poetry, Who nearer to me Or more mighty yes, more mighty than I Tore me away from myself. Tore me away!" Everything depends on the language, on the living author's struggle with a past artist's words and on the future reader's ability to hold in mind two opposed meanings—*O Dio* and odium, heaven and repugnance. A capacity for imaginative projection into the lifeworld, thought, and language of another person, whether living or dead, through music, literature, the visual arts, or conversation—this is the ethical burden of agapē in the arts.

The Self Who Could Do (No) More

The theme of a nearer, "more mighty" self had a grip on Gaddis, obviously. And although he cites many models in history and in literature—Socrates, Michelangelo, Glenn Gould, Tolstoy, Wyatt Gwyon in his own novel *The Recognitions*—at the end of his life he was preoccupied with one "exalted friend"[9] and mentor, who had been crucial to his work on *The Recognitions*. Martin S. Dworkin was in the fifties a widely published critic, photographer, and editor who pushed Gaddis, himself unpublished, to a higher standard. Those who knew Dworkin and Gaddis estimate that as many as thirty-eight of their conversations found their way into *The Recognitions*.[10] The conversations continued, on paper, a full two years after Dworkin's death in 1996.

In notes Gaddis made while concluding his final fiction, Dworkin appears as both an "enabler" and an "accuser," an intense teacher whose intellectual generosity exacted a psychic toll: "that was always his thing, the accuser, you've let me down, you've betrayed me; my 'dialogues' with him (he talked) were so important to me to feeling able to do what I did (REC) unafraid." Dworkin was always older—only by three or four years but "an overwhelming difference" in the prime of creative development: "Those years were packed with his mind, his lust for knowing everything." This one-sided dialogue finds its answering voice in the fiction. The intensity of a lifelong conversation gets carried forward into old age, and the shared thoughts promise to survive death, because these men really believed—they were creatively driven by the faith—that literature and the arts were the place where a few unique minds could meet in a kind of fellowship.

Although the material on Dworkin never found its way

into the final draft of *Agapē Agape,* Gaddis preserved a conversational impulse similar to what had seen him through the composition of *The Recognitions.* Feeling a "need to speak with those no longer here" (as he wrote in his notes), Gaddis this time channeled his thoughts into a series of imaginary conversations—Walter Benjamin in dialogue with Johan Huizinga, Nietzsche communing with himself in his final mad days spent mostly improvising on the piano, and the man on the bed in direct conversation with various characters from fiction: Svengali (from *Trilby*), Hoffmann (from Offenbach's posthumously published *Tales*), Pózdnyshev (from *The Kreutzer Sonata*). In each case music, the art most conducive to unspoken fellowship, is the medium and occasion for the conversation. Its appreciation is best expressed by two people listening and keeping quiet for as long as the music lasts. But the agitations that such listening might cause were understood by Tolstoy, an author whose role as a secular prophet dismayed Gaddis but whose work he never ceased quoting. Music in *The Kreutzer Sonata* is a source of dangerous emotional and physical connection. Tolstoy's narrator, Pózdnyshev, complains that piano recitals initiated "the greater part of the adulteries in our society."[11] But music is also recognized as creating a separate place where one experiences emotions and sensations that are less easily defined:

"How can I put it? Music makes me forget myself, my real position; it transports me to some other position not my own. Under the influence of music it seems to me that I feel what I do not really feel, that I understand what I do not understand, that I can do what I cannot do. . . . Music carries me immediately and directly into the mental condition in which the man was who composed it. My soul merges with his and together with him I pass from one condition into another, but why this happens I don't know."[12]

The experience Pózdnyshev struggles to define is neither exaltation nor entertainment. It is something akin, rather, to the mental communion enacted by Gaddis in *Agapē Agape*. Against all forgeries, simulations, and wastes of the world, this was the one consolation that Gaddis held on to during the last stages of composition: that the life of the mind in collaboration with other minds, the fraternal love that he felt in his recollection of a friend no longer here, and the disciplined recognition of the achievements of past writers would give to his work a staying power beyond his own, finally human, powers of caring and invention.

Notes

1. Tom LeClair, *The Art of Excess: Mastery in Contemporary American Fiction* (Urbana: University of Illinois Press, 1989).

2. As told to Matthew Gaddis, who did some minor secretarial work for his father during the years when Gaddis worked on the player-piano essay and the fiction that evolved out of it.

3. *Concrete*, trans. David McLintock (Chicago: University of Chicago Press, 1984), p. 3.

4. As told to Matthew Gaddis.

5. *Paris Review,* Winter 1987, p. 71.

6. Ibid., pp. 71–72.

7. Patrick O'Donnell, "His Master's Voice: Commodifying Identity in *J R,*" in *Echo Chambers: Figuring Voice in Modern Narrative* (Iowa City: University of Iowa Press, 1992), p. 176.

8. "O Heaven, Heaven, Heaven!
   Who's robbed me of myself
   Who's closer to myself
   Or can do more with me than I ever can?"

Complete Poems and Selected Letters of Michelangelo, trans. Creighton Gilbert (New York: Random House, 1963), p. 7.

9. From Gaddis's working papers.

10. "Martin S. Dworkin: His Life and Work," http://members.aol.com/ _ht_a/flobern/my homepage/

11. Leo Tolstoy, "The Kreutzer Sonata," in Tolstoy, *Collected Shorter Fiction*, trans. Louise and Aylmer Maude and Nigel J. Cooper (New York: Alfred A. Knopf, 2001), p. 299.

12. Ibid.,

FOR THE BEST IN PAPERBACKS, LOOK FOR THE ⓟ

In every corner of the world, on every subject under the sun, Penguin represents quality and variety—the very best in publishing today.

For complete information about books available from Penguin—including Penguin Classics, Penguin Compass, and Puffins—and how to order them, write to us at the appropriate address below. Please note that for copyright reasons the selection of books varies from country to country.

In the United States: Please write to *Penguin Group (USA), P.O. Box 12289 Dept. B, Newark, New Jersey 07101-5289* or call 1-800-788-6262.

In the United Kingdom: Please write to *Dept. EP, Penguin Books Ltd, Bath Road, Harmondsworth, West Drayton, Middlesex UB7 0DA.*

In Canada: Please write to *Penguin Books Canada Ltd, 10 Alcorn Avenue, Suite 300, Toronto, Ontario M4V 3B2.*

In Australia: Please write to *Penguin Books Australia Ltd, P.O. Box 257, Ringwood, Victoria 3134.*

In New Zealand: Please write to *Penguin Books (NZ) Ltd, Private Bag 102902, North Shore Mail Centre, Auckland 10.*

In India: Please write to *Penguin Books India Pvt Ltd, 11 Panchsheel Shopping Centre, Panchsheel Park, New Delhi 110 017.*

In the Netherlands: Please write to *Penguin Books Netherlands bv, Postbus 3507, NL-1001 AH Amsterdam.*

In Germany: Please write to *Penguin Books Deutschland GmbH, Metzlerstrasse 26, 60594 Frankfurt am Main.*

In Spain: Please write to *Penguin Books S. A., Bravo Murillo 19, 1° B, 28015 Madrid.*

In Italy: Please write to *Penguin Italia s.r.l., Via Benedetto Croce 2, 20094 Corsico, Milano.*

In France: Please write to *Penguin France, Le Carré Wilson, 62 rue Benjamin Baillaud, 31500 Toulouse.*

In Japan: Please write to *Penguin Books Japan Ltd, Kaneko Building, 2-3-25 Koraku, Bunkyo-Ku, Tokyo 112.*

In South Africa: Please write to *Penguin Books South Africa (Pty) Ltd, Private Bag X14, Parkview, 2122 Johannesburg.*

CLICK ON A CLASSIC
www.penguinclassics.com

The world's greatest literature at your fingertips

Constantly updated information on more than a thousand titles,
from Icelandic sagas to ancient Indian epics, Russian drama to
Italian romance, American greats to African masterpieces

•

The latest news on recent additions to the list, updated
editions, and specially commissioned translations

•

Original essays by leading writers

•

A wealth of background material, including biographies
of every classic author from Aristotle to Zamyatin, plot
synopses, readers' and teachers' guides, useful web links

•

Online desk and examination copy assistance for academics

•

Trivia quizzes, competitions, giveaways, news on
forthcoming screen adaptations

Printed in the United States
by Baker & Taylor Publisher Services